I0724531

OUTBACK YANKEE

THE VERY PUBLIC DISAPPEARANCE OF MARINA SHENKO

EBONY MCKENNA

Sunlight cast prison bars of light through the timber shutters. Dust tickled her nose. A tremor of semi-worry tension grew between Marina's shoulder blades.

How to describe this new dorm she stood in? Boutique? Compact? Cozy? *Cramped.* The thought "I'm going to die in this tiny room. Unmourned, untweeted," wriggled through her brain.

Before today, influencer and *It Gal* Marina Shenko had never truly appreciated how much jetlag could mess with a person's head. Woozy confusion took hold as she tried her utmost to be as polite as possible in the face of *extreme* adversity.

Hand reaching for her cell phone, she found an empty pocket. Drat. It must be somewhere in her bags. Without it, she couldn't tell her followers that she really, honestly, hand-on-the-heart, promise-to-God wasn't deliberately vanishing off the face of the earth as a kooky publicity stunt.

The moment she got her cell back, she'd make it up to her fans. They needed to hear from her regularly, or they'd forget about her. Being forgotten didn't bear thinking about.

May as well cut out my tongue!

An earlier tremor of *not-yet-panic* brought a friend along. Together they made a *but-we-are-very-close-to-getting-there* ripple up her spine.

Marina shook it off with an attempt at humor. "Well, this is crap!"

The woman standing beside her clicked her tongue and said in an almost-British accent, "Language, *please.* We are ladies here at Boomerang Estate."

Marina mournfully sighed. Her fingers, so used to tapping on a screen, flickered and flailed for something to touch. She reached for the wall and caught her hand on a long cord with a bobble at the end. It pulled with a jarring clunk. Light filled the room, shining on two single beds. Each was burdened with fiercely floral covers, lace pillows and overflowing pastel ruffles.

Those little ripples of fear in her muscles started to rumble. *Breathe in, one two three. Breathe out one two three.* No good. Her thumbs twitched. "Can I have my cell back please?"

"Digital devices are only permitted as a reward for good behavior. You'll need to earn your privileges –"

"– Please give it back." Those rumbles in her back

migrated to her belly. *Is this what withdrawal symptoms feel like for an addict?* "You have to give it back. It's mine!"

"Lower your voice, Miss Marina, shouting is most unladylike."

Breathing through the panic, pushing it down to her feet, she tried again. "I need my cell. My fans will be going crazy with worry."

The woman remained in the doorway, blocking Marina's exit. "Your parents have sent you here for a very good reason. Please respect their decision and the rules of Boomerang Estate."

Her foggy brain They could dress the place up with whatever fancy name they wanted, but the lady was kidding herself if this *estate* was anything other than a brat camp for anti-social teens. What horrible thing had she done to deserve this kind of evil punishment? *I'm one of the good ones!*

Her parents had never worried about her internet profile before. If anything, they'd encouraged it. Daddy had called her '*My little Internet-preneur*'. Yet they were punishing her with exile to the other side of the planet? For what? And while her brain was riffing on the subject, where were Marina's parents? It was all a bit fuzzy, but Marina was sure her Mom had been in the taxi that brought her here.

The woman standing beside her pursed her lips, breathed slowly and then said with a dismissive tone, "We've had a great many girls undergo digital detoxification. Granted, it takes some adjustment, but you'll get used to it soon enough. We'll send your belongings up."

"I'm not *addicted*. It's my job, Beatrice!" Marina said. This lady wasn't getting it. "I know *some* people are addicted to their phones, but I *need* to use mine all the time because I'm a *brand*. Social media is my career! I'm an influencer. I've got fans all over the world. Probably here in Australia too. Fans who *need* me! Do you have any idea what being offline *even for a day* will do to my social currency?"

So whiney! What a terrible first impression Marina must be making. Blame those trembling, nerves running through her system with glee. And jet-lag. The flight from the States had taken forever and a day. And somewhere along the line her mother had put her in a taxi but somehow not joined in. It was all so fuzzy. How long had she been offline now?

The woman blinked slowly. "It's Miss Beatrice, and the rules are for all. Everybody is here for a different reason, but we follow the same rules."

"Give me a moment," Marina crouched onto the floor, searching under the beds for a wall socket. The moment she had her cell back, she'd charge it up.

Miss Beatrice cleared her throat. "It is unladylike to contort yourself in such a fashion."

A shaft of light illuminated the dust motes, highlighting the chipped varnish on the bed legs, the tatty ends of the floor rug, thick dust on the skirting boards and scuffs on Miss Beatrice's shoes. Something glistened in a gap in the wood. She swept her fingers over the floor and grabbed it. A clip-on earring. Marina stood up and handed it over. "Is this yours?"

"How odd." Miss Beatrice took the piece between her thumb and finger. "I shall see if I have the matching pair in my jewel box. Thank you for your honesty."

"Does that earn privileges?"

She smiled. "Continued honesty and good behavior will take you far."

Marina shuffled over to the window and opened the shutters. It had been the usual, mild Californian winter when she'd left home. Heat blasted her in the face as she lifted the sash. Outside was a blindingly stark, orange landscape, dotted with grey-green trees and shrubby-looking things. An off-brand Wild West, with dust swirling around straggly plants near a wire fence.

She shut the window to keep the heat out. Too much for her tired brain to process. Luckily, there was a bed right beside her, so she flopped onto it. It creaked like a rusty gate. "Oh God. Mom really hates me."

Miss Beatrice tilted her head to the side. "Your parents love you very much. That's why you're here."

What a stupid way to show love. "If they really loved me, they'd want me to be happy and I am the complete opposite of happy right now."

"Give it time, Miss Marina."

An enormous sigh escaped. "Yes Beatrice." She had to get back online. But how?

"It's *Miss* Beatrice," Miss Beatrice corrected.

"Yes, *Miss* Beatrice." An idea sparked. When her suitcases arrived, she'd grab her phone and credit cards and head into town, then find a way back to a major airport. Something told her *Miss* Beatrice wouldn't be too forthcoming with directions, but she'd find a way.

Miss Beatrice continued. "Once you have put away your personal items from your handbag you may join us in the reading room."

"I need to unpack my brain." Rusty metal squeaks filled the room as she wriggled on the bed. No way would she get any rest in this one. She tested the other bed; it was just as bad. If she lay still, the squeaking eventually stopped. Lying still with so much worry surging through her was impossible, so the *squeakage* resumed. "Am I allowed to take a walk outside later?"

"Provided you have no outstanding duties, you may take a stroll, accompanied by another resident. For your own safety, of course. We are quite isolated here and we take bushfire and other warnings seriously. Spider and snake bites can and do kill."

"Is there anything in Australia that doesn't want to kill me?"

Miss Beatrice gave a knowing smile, "We are a good way from the coast, so at least you needn't worry yourself about sharks."

Something clattered on the roof. Marina sat up in shock.

"Probably magpies landing," Miss Beatrice said. "Corrugated iron roofs tend to amplify the sound.

Magpies are only dangerous in Spring, they generally don't want to swoop and gouge your eyes out at this time of year."

Was that supposed to be reassuring?

Then something altogether new and strange *boomf'd* on the window.

Then *boomf*. There it was again, leaving a clump of dirt on the window pane. Marina and Miss Beatrice looked at each other in confusion.

Boomf.

Marina pulled the sash open. "Hold your fire!"

A convenient distraction, roughly the same age as Marina, appeared on the dusty ground outside. Orange dirt creased his deeply tanned face. When he smiled his white teeth dazzled in the sun.

"Hello there, diversion." Marina leaned on the windowsill. "Are you a lucky resident of Boomerang Estate too?"

"Come away from the window," Miss Beatrice gripped Marina's upper arm.

From this distance, he looked kind of hot. Solid jaw, tanned and windblown from being out in the elements. Hair? No idea, hidden under one of those brown not-quite-cowboy hats. His squinting made discerning his eye color tricky.

"Come away and close the shutters, no fraternizing with staff." That was Miss Beatrice again. Honestly, the woman lived for rules. Weren't Australians supposed to be easy going and laid back? When they weren't wrestling crocodiles. She pointed to the guy on the ground. "And you, young man, can get away from the window thank you very much."

He shrugged and said, "The boomerang landed on the roof." He made all the right facial expressions for someone contrite. In his drawling accent he said, "I'm showing the girls the right way but not all of them are getting it."

"Ladies," Miss Beatrice corrected. "You're instructing the *ladies*."

"Yeah, that too. I was tryna get the maggies to get it down for me," he said.

A giggle escaped Marina's throat. He sounded *adorable*!

"I hardly see how throwing clods of soil will achieve that. Retrieve a ladder from storage to get the boomerang down. Hold your instructions farther from the main building in future."

"No worries," he said.

"Do you live here too?" Marina called out, ignoring Miss Beatrice's exhortations to close the shutters and step away, as if simply talking to a boy would somehow break the very fabric of space and time. And possibly moral decency.

Miss Beatrice's voice rose an octave. "If you're quite finished with this incessant *flirting*!" Anyone would think she'd walked in on them having sex. "Young man, hurry up and retrieve your sports equipment and kindly leave."

Marina leaned half way out the window. "What's your name?"

"Cooper. What's yours?"

"Marina Shenko."

His broad smile played over her like a cool drink of soda.

"Miss Marina, that is *enough!*" Miss Beatrice pulled her bodily into the room with one arm and pulled the window sash closed with the other. Then she slapped the shutters together. The light shone through the vertical slits in the wood, bringing back that prison bar look. "There is to be no flirting."

"Lighten up, B. He's just a boy." No big deal. It wasn't as if he was going to ravish them in their sleep. Not that Marina completely understood the meaning of ravish. She'd heard it in a podcast and liked how it rhymed with *lavish*.

"Your fellow resident, Miss Pearl, requires rest and privacy, so you are not to be making her excited or agitated."

Miss Pearl sounded like she might be eighty-years-old. Why a senior needed digital detox was anyone's guess. Just to be sure, Marina sniffed. No tell-tale chicken-soup-and-urine smell in the air, so her parents hadn't booked her into an aged care home by mistake.

As soon as the rest of her bags arrived, she'd be going through them superfast to find her cell. And the spare. Of course, she had a second one. Nobody with her profile relied on just the one. "Where's the games room?"

There were bound to be wall sockets there, so she could charge them up as well.

"There is a library in the south wing, you are welcome to avail yourself of any titles on the shelves."

That would be a 'no' then. Marina had to make contact and let her fans know she was OK. They must be going crazy with worry. On the other hand ... *No, don't think about that.* Too late, the thought popped in her head anyway. The thought that her fans had forgotten all about her and moved on to whoever else was putting up a cute video or posting selfies surrounded by amazing artwork. Losing her followers sent panic sprites through her system.

Miss Beatrice cast Marina a sympathetic smile. "I know it will take some adjustment, but it will be for your own good. I shall see you downstairs soon."

The moment she'd gone, Marina checked once more for sockets – even inside the wardrobe – but came up empty-handed. Maybe the estate pre-dated electricity? Frustration brought heat to her eyes, but she stopped herself and willed those self-pity-white-girl-tears away. She shook out her arms and legs and took a few breaths. She might be exiled to *The Upside Down*, but she would never be down and out.

Waiting for her cases left her at the mercy of Miss Beatrice. Best get them herself. The worn carpet runner in the hall barely cushioned her feet. The oak balustrade was worn smooth from decades of wear. Noted and *noted.*

Fortune smiled on her. The suitcases were exactly where the cab driver had left them just inside the front door. She extended their handles and strolled back to the stairs.

"One moment, Miss Marina." Miss Beatrice bustled into the scene.

"It's all right, I'm doing it myself."

"We must check your belongings for contraband before we return them to you."

You're what? "I don't think so!"

"House rules."

No way! The wheels *boffed* against the steps as Marina stomped up to her room.

"Miss Marina, stop this nonsense." Beatrice lunged for the luggage.

"Let go!" Marina yelled.

"Don't make a scene!"

People actually said that? "There's nobody here!" Making her a liar, a group of young women stepped into the front hall and looked up to them.

"Please leave your belongings on the landing and come down where I shall make introductions."

The other women looked about Marina's age. What horrible crimes had they committed to end up here?

"Hey everyone, I'm Marina and I'm taking my stuff into my room." She gave a mighty pull on the handles and headed off. The rest of the prisoners, sorry, *residents*, could wait.

Once in her room, Marina closed the door – no lock,

of course – and emptied everything onto the bed. Clothes tumbled out. Power cords, adaptors, battery rechargers, ear buds and headphones followed. But no phone.

The pockets! These cases had so many pockets and sections; so easy to forget. She searched every one of them. Even unzipping the lining to see if anything had somehow fallen between it and the outer casing.

Damn! Fighting rising panic, she re-checked every single pocket and came away with nothing but sore fingers from scraping the bottom of the figurative barrel. Had Beatrice already been through her cases and taken everything out?

Had her parents?

She pulled jeans, sweaters, and scarves out of the way. Judging by the heat outside, she wouldn't be needing the winter wardrobe any time soon. Mom must have done a Penn and Teller and distracted her at some point, because Marina was certain she'd packed two cell-phones. *Uh-oh.* Credit cards and passport; also missing. Everything went fuzzy as she absorbed the utter brutality of her situation.

A knock came to the door. A woman about Marina's age came in. She had fine blonde hair and seriously pale skin that would utterly frizzle in that harsh sun outside. All British-accented and cute as a button.

"Sorry to bother you. Miss Beatrice sent me up to fetch you for afternoon tea. I'm Pearl. I mean, *Miss Pearl.* We'll be sharing this room."

This was Pearl? "Miss Pearl, do you have a cell phone?"

"Sorry, Miss Beatrice confiscated it when I arrived."

"You too huh?"

"None of us has, if that's what you're asking. We're all here on detox."

What the hell kind of place is this? "How old are you?"

"I'm eighteen," Pearl said. "How about you?"

"What? You're an adult, you can leave any time you like?"

Miss Pearl smiled and shrugged. "I want to be here. The peace and quiet is exactly what I need. I take it you're younger?"

"Yeah. Sixteen."

"Are you missing school?"

Time zones twisted in Marina's brain. "We're just about to head into midwinter recess so," she shrugged. "I guess I'm here for a week maybe? You know what? Maybe if I'm here for only a week I might be OK?"

Pearl smiled but said nothing.

Fear swooped through Marina's stomach. "I won't be out of here in a week, will I?

"It depends what your parents have selected for you."

Marina slumped on her bed, filling the room with squeaks and groans from the rusty springs. "How long are you in for?"

"My case is a little different," Pearl said, looking at her shoes.

Marina sucked the inside of her cheek in thought. "You have strict parents too?"

Pearl made a shy smile. "I'm here for the peace and quiet."

That set Marina back. Peace and quiet was getting massages at a spa and posting glamour shots on Instafeed, not stuck here in the dusty outback. "I know this is incredibly rude of me and we've just met, but can I borrow some money? I'm totally good for it and as soon as I get a cell I'll get on a network and transfer money into your account."

Pearl blushed and said, "I don't have access to any money . . . at the moment."

"That's probably why *The B* made you my roommate. I can't slip up if you can't give me cash."

Pearl shrugged. "Something like that. Anyway, we're due for afternoon tea, let's get down there."

'Afternoon Tea' consisted of everyone meeting in the library, a room with oversized leather chairs with scuffs and cracks in the arms. There were about a dozen girls in here, forming a line to take a cup and saucer from a side table. One by one they poured themselves hot black tea from a pot, then moved further down the table and added milk and sugar.

No lemon? How strange.

Tea came with a small sugar cookie, which everyone insisted on calling a 'biscuit'.

"Ladies, today we shall discuss anti-social behavior," Miss Beatrice said.

Marina huffed out a breath, then inwardly freaked when nobody else did. They must have been here for a while already, judging by their compliance.

One of the girls leaned forward and placed her cup on the floor, before sitting back and crossing her arms. Good move. Marina did the same.

"There is no need to be defensive," Miss Beatrice said, looking around the room at the glaringly obvious body language from some of them. "Afternoon Tea is every afternoon for the length of your stay. The more you share, the more you benefit." Her gaze came to rest on a girl wearing the most gorgeous sari. The threads sparkled as she crossed her legs under the long skirt. Beautiful outfit, but it made her a target.

"Miss Prithee, would you start please? What would be considered anti-social behavior to you?"

Prithee looked up, her mouth in a tight line, as if she didn't want to talk. Protective anger surged in Marina. "You better not be picking on her just because she's . . . where are you from?" Marina said. Oh, hang on, was *that* anti-social? But still, she was glad she'd stood up for the girl.

"You mistake my pause for reticence," Prithee said as

she turned to Marina. "I am able to speak for myself, and I'm *from* Australia."

Red hot embarrassment roared up Marina's neck and face. "Sorry," squeaked out. *Could the ground please open up and swallow me?*

Prithee's smile filled with satisfaction as she looked back to Miss Beatrice. "Not getting along could be considered by some to be anti-social. But the true nature of anti-social is defined by personal circumstances and social mores and customs of the culture you find yourself in," she said. "For example, in Mongolian culture, when it comes to eating, it's polite to place the entire small parcel of food inside your mouth at one time. Taking a bite of your food and removing the rest from your mouth is considered disgusting."

Mongolia? But Prithee said she was –

"– In other cultures, it's considered anti-social to defy your parents and not meet their expectations."

Lots of nodding happened around the circle. Marina joined in, because she didn't want to be singled out. As she looked around the room, she noticed Pearl wasn't there. Uptight Pearl totally wasn't the kind of girl to break the rules.

"Let's bring it in from the abstract to the practical," Miss Beatrice said, "Let's go around the room and describe ways in which you have been anti-social, and what you could do to improve your behaviour."

Marina needed her cup of tea again, to form a barrier

across herself. As she reached down, one of the girls began to talk in a thick Australian accent.

"Everyone knows I had a big night and my parents had to come and get me from the cops. Again."

Marina didn't know, but then she barely even knew what part of Australia she was in. The limo drive from the airport had taken forever, so they had to be somewhere in The Outback, right?

One of the girls made a thumbs-up gesture to the confessed drunk and said, "That's not anti-social, that's a normal weekend."

Laughter filled the room. The shelves of densely packed books absorbed the sounds.

"Miss Taylah, *please*," Miss Beatrice said.

Pretending to take a sip of her tea, Marina glanced towards Taylah. She had a cheeky charm about her. Scrubbed clean of makeup, the stretched hole in her lower earlobe and the dents in the side of her nose and eyebrow were all that remained of her decorative piercings.

They must have hurt! And also, those piercings must have really annoyed her parents. Maybe that was why she was here? Also? They should definitely be friends.

The unstirred sugar in the bottom of her cup gave Marina a welcome boost of sweetness. She raised her hand.

"Yes, Miss Marina, you wish to add to the conversation?" Miss Beatrice asked.

In truth, Marina hadn't even listened to most of the

conversation. "I am sorry for interrupting, but um, could somebody show me to the restroom?"

"We call them toilets here," Taylah said.

Ooooh, perfect. Marina's body responded with a warm blush. And now that she'd said the word, her bladder came along to the party. "I guess you'll need to bring me up to speed on understanding Australian."

"Miss Taylah," Miss Beatrice said, "Kindly show Miss Marina the way."

"No worries Miss."

Perfect, perfect, perfect! Placing her empty cup and saucer on the serving table, Marina followed the young woman down the hall.

Taylah grinned to Marina and kept her voice low. "Didja really need to go, or didja jus' need to get outta there?"

She barely understood the girl, but Marina desperately needed a friend here so she smiled and nodded and then shrugged, because Taylah was looking at her, expecting an answer. Pointing to the door behind her, she said, "Is this it?"

"Yep. I'm s'posed to come in and make sure you don't do a runner, then walk you back. But listening to someone take a slash isn't my idea of fun, so I'll just wait out 'ere."

Drat. The bathroom had no windows. No chance to climb out. In any case, now that she was here, she used the facilities and washed her hands.

Exiting to the hall, she found Taylah leaning in to the

wall, her neck bent at a familiar angle. Whisper shouting, she said, "Ohmigoshyou'vegotacellphone!"

"Shh!" Taylah tucked it into her bra and then grabbed Marina by the wrist. "Don't say a bloody word."

Marina shook her head and made a zipping motion over her closed mouth with her free hand. Then she immediately unzipped it and whispered. "Have you got a signal?"

"Nah. Wind's blowing the wrong way."

That made zero sense, but Marina wasn't going to labor the point. "I have to post an update right now to let people know I'm still alive."

"Are you in WitPro too?"

"*What?* No. I'm Marina Shenko." What the heck was 'witpro' anyway?

Taylah replied with a blank look.

"The *NoozPoster*?" Marina prompted.

Still nothing.

"Come on, you must have NoozPost in Australia?"

"Course we have. Are you s'posed to be famous or somethin'?"

Marina sighed.

"Only kidding. I know who you are. Wanna bust out of this pl –?"

"– You bet!"

Taylah grinned and tilted her head towards the front door. "Let's go then."

A few seconds later, Marina and Taylah were out the front door, onto the wide porch amongst the pots of geraniums that were baking in the heat. The late afternoon sky bleached her retinas.

Freedom and reconnection with the outside world beckoned.

Marina squinted. "I should have brought my sunglasses." Then she looked back to the homestead to make sure Miss Beatrice wasn't following them.

"Yep," Taylah said. "Sun's got a real kick in it." A tray truck drove up from behind them. "Our ride's here. Hop in."

To Marina's delight, a smiling Cooper sat behind the wheel. The wheel was on the wrong side of the car though, which piled more confusion onto her already frazzled brain.

"Two tickets into town, good sir," Taylah said, climbing in and sliding along the bench seat into to the middle. Marina climbed in and pulled the door shut. She had absolutely no idea where they'd end up, but at least she was certain of two things.

Both Taylah and Cooper had cellphones.

And wherever they were going, it had to be better than Boomerang Brat Camp.

CHAPTER TWO

"Whaddya mean your account's blocked?" Cooper said as he slid opposite Marina into the cafe booth.

Cold clamminess made Marina's fingers slip on the touchscreen. Fresh-brewed panic had her typing the wrong password. "I'm trying again." Which she did. The stress of hitting the wrong keys blurred her vision. *So not fair. So completely utterly, horribly not fair.* "It has to be the jetlag. I can't type properly."

On the fifteen-minute drive to this small town, Marina had borrowed Cooper's cell and made several unsuccessful attempts to log in to her accounts. She blamed her failures on the bumpy road and twinges of carsickness. Yet now they were seated in a little diner, with no bumping and a steady table to lean on, there was no valid reason why she couldn't log in.

Taylah said, "Sure it is," as she sat herself beside Marina.

"I just have to breathe and relax. I'll get this fixed and pay for the meal like I said I would."

"Ten bucks says they've blocked your accounts." Taylah added.

A bucket of cold water couldn't have doused Marina faster. Which sure was something, given the hot conditions. Surely her parents weren't so cruel as to cut off her income? Unfortunately, the more she tried – and slowed her breathing and tried again, really slowly this time – the more she had to accept her accounts were no longer hers to access. The reality of her situation clenched her stomach.

"Same thing happened to me," Taylah said. "To rub salt in the wound, they cut off my *Instafeed* as well."

Stomach roiling, Marina hit a familiar app on Cooper's phone and looked up her name.

"This account is currently blocked."

"Oh, come on!"

If it had been her device, she would have thrown it clear across the room.

No money. No social media access. The only good thing right now was that Marina had no food in her stomach, so she couldn't throw up.

"Call your olds," Cooper said.

"Pardon?"

"Your old folks, your parents. Give 'em a call."

If she'd been holding her own phone, she would

have. But her family contacts weren't in this one, and in her frazzled, stressed-out state, she couldn't remember the numbers.

"Hang on, ya gotta call out of the country first," Taylah said, taking the phone and searching for a page to show how to dial international numbers. "This looks good. OK, you're calling from Australia, to America, and here's some California prefixes and now you put the number in. What's the phone number?"

Utterly blank. Marina's mind shut down. Hoping to jog her memory, she tapped her thumb against her fingers, creating a pattern. Closing her eyes helped, and she spoke the numbers out loud.

"Is this right?" Taylah held the screen up.

"Yeah, I think so," Marina took the phone and held it to her ear.

It rang! A smile spread on her face as she thought about what nice things she'd say to Daddy. The soft one. She'd talk him round to reneging on whatever deal he and Mom had made to punish her. Not that she even knew what she'd done to deserve this kind of punishment.

Having a social media career that earned her money through advertising and clothing sponsorships was just as valid a career as her father selling paintings and sculptures by other people. Half of her selfies were with the up-for-auction artworks in the background anyway. Their careers fed each other.

When it came down to it, they were both promoting other people's products.

The phone kept ringing. "That's odd, it should have gone to voicemail by now."

Cooper said, "Time zones and all that. It could be the middle of the night."

The phone kept ringing. And ringing.

Finally, it clicked off. "I'll send him a message," she tapped her thumbs on the keyboard. "Miss you Daddy. Brat Camp is bratty. Hugs to Mom and baby bro."

Why hadn't Dad answered? He was always taking calls. Even in the middle of the night. Especially leading up to the monthly sales. At those times, his cell was permanently attached to his head day and night.

She rang back. The line clicked and bleeped. A compressed digital voice said, *'The number you have called is not connected to any networks.'*

The what now? Stress levels rising, Marina steadied her breathing. Closing her eyes again, she recalled Mom's number and dialed. The moment her mother answered she'd ask what the hell was going on. The same thing happened though. A few rings, then that irritating message about the number not being connected.

"Everything OK?" Cooper asked.

"No." There was only one thing for it, she had to call her kid brother. "They're playing mind games, I just know it."

Brady answered before the first ring finished, his

voice barely above a whisper. "There's nobody here," he said.

"Hey kiddo it's me. You'll never believe it but I'm in Australia! What's up?"

"Reena!" His voice was muffled, as if talking through a towel. "Stay away from the house, it's crawling with agents. I'm a minor, they can't charge me with anything."

"Ha-ha, yeah, and I bet there's a few aliens as well."

"I'm serious, stay away. And you can't call me either, I was just about to flush my cell."

"Have you been at Mom's tablets again?"

"I gotta go, they're on the stairs."

The phone went dead. Irritation had Marina dialing straight back, only to get a *'this number is not switched on or is out of range,'* message.

"He is such a pest!" Marina put the phone down. Her brother was always pulling pranks. Last time they'd talked he'd said, "I can only tell you what the Moogins tell me." Classic annoying kid brother.

An idea pinged. Her social accounts might be closed, but her friends still had theirs. She found Sophie's virtual doorbell avatar and rang it. "It's Marina, but my accounts are all closed so I'll have to start a new one." She leaned in to get a selfie with Taylah but the other girl leaned out of the way, "Nah, I hate photos."

"Cooper?"

Taylah laughed, "You'll steal his spirit."

"– What? –"

"– Don't start." Cooper shook his head.

"Hey Sophie, it's Marina, I have a new cell . . . and I'm in Outback Australia!"

Barely a half-minute passed before Sophie replied with her own direct message:

"OMG!!!!! Mari, is that you!!!!!?"

Marina typed back: *"The 1 and only."*

"Where have you been? You vanished off the face of the earth gf!!! Is this about the parentals? They are totally in the news right now!!!!!!!!!!"

Fear curdled Marina's stomach. Why would her parents be making the news? Unless they'd achieved a record price for something? But sale day wasn't for a while yet.

"WTF?"

"It's all over ZMZ babe!!!!! Switch it on!!!!!!!!"

Cooper's hand pressed over the screen. "Don't tell her where you are."

Bit late for that. "Sophie says my parents are on ZMZ."

"Hang on," Cooper took the phone back and tapped at it, then held the screen for Marina to see ZMZ's home page. It wasn't the first item, that was default space reserved for the ultrafamous. But it was there, a little further down the list.

"Police raid Shenko palazzo after celebs cry foul on bogus Banksy."

She was definitely clicking on that! But the more Marina read, the more her stomach buckled with fear and confusion. The article mentioned several A-list celebrities who'd paid top dollar at auction but now wanted their money back. This had to be some kind of terrible misunderstanding. People in the spotlight would do or say anything to stay there. Complaining to the media was like a daily fix for some of them, especially the faded ones.

There couldn't be any truth in it.

But the optics of detectives coming out of her family home in Brentwood with huge paper evidence bags? Terrible!

"Maybe this is why your parents sent you here," Cooper said.

"God, what a mess." Marina wasn't sure if she'd said the words out loud.

The only thing she was sure about?

The bottom had just fallen out of her world.

Looking through the windows of the café, the late afternoon light burned the ground into a glorious orange, contrasting with the fierce blue sky. A view wasted on Marina as she crouched at the table, body trembling with shock, eyes losing focus. Something was going very, very wrong back home and here she was on the other side of the world, unable to do anything about it.

Utterly powerless.

Unless . . . maybe this explained her exile? Her parents must have sent her away to protect her. That had to be it. All the same, they could have found a nicer way of doing it? Or at least given her a heads-up.

Her parents must have known something was coming, that's why her mother had flown all the way over here with her, even climbed into the cab with her and paid the driver. They were so sleepy from the long flight.

So groggy. No, wait. Marina was the groggy one. Her mother had been super focused and alert.

Marina couldn't even remember making it through the passport checks. And she was sure her mother had sat in the back of the cab with her, but then, wait ... it wasn't adding up. The last thing she was sure of was waking up in the back of a cab at Boomerang Estate.

None of it made sense.

A yawn crashed out, followed by another.

Cooper let out a hearty laugh and said, "You are so screwed. No phone and no money. Whatja do? Run over someone's Nan?"

Sarcasm came to Marina's defense. "Thank you for your understanding."

With a shrug, he said, "If you're worried about money, I can take care of it."

"Wait a minute, I haven't tried *MunneeBud*," she virtually squeezed the device and downloaded the app. Spin, spin, spin – the progress circle took its sweet time! "Omigod it's working!" Light filled her veins. Why hadn't she thought of this earlier and saved herself the heartache? Because she was jetlagged and wasn't thinking straight, that's why. Hope soared as she put in her password (amazing that she even remembered it) and the app gave a 'welcome back' chime.

Yes, yes, yes!

Her hopes crashed at the sight of her balance.

Zero dollars.

Accompanied by a sad face emoji.

Beyond brutal!

"They have to be pranking me," Marina tried to salvage a scrap of dignity. "There must be cameras here. Any minute now they're going to leap out and laugh at me." Except her family were in Los Angeles and people were raiding their house.

The waitress came over with three plates of food balanced on her arms. "He ya go loves."

"Thank you," Marina replied, placing the phone on the table. She had no appetite, and no clue what was on her plate. Something wrapped in pastry and a huge serving of thick-cut fries.

"It's a pie, love. It won't bite ya," the waitress said.

"Oh, please excuse me, I didn't mean to be rude. What sort of pie is it?" It was impossible to tell from the pastry covering the top. It lacked the tell-tale sweetness of cherry or apple.

"Oh, you're American," the waitress's smile grew by twenty per cent. "You're in for a treat. This is our award-winning chicken and veggie supreme. Best pies this side of Sydney."

Barely understanding a word of it, Marina offered a wonky smile in return "That's nice."

Beside her, Taylah squeezed ketchup from a plastic red bottle all over the surface of her pie. Cooper picked his pie up in one hand and bit straight in.

Marina took her knife and fork and pierced the top, releasing a plume of savory aromas. "It's like a thick stew, in pastry," she said, eyeing the chunks of white meat, gravy, peas and minced carrots. A tentative bite and all felt good. Another mouthful and it was as if the food hugged her from the inside. "This is good! How have I not had one of these until now?"

It didn't solve her problem of having no phone, money or passport. It didn't explain what was going on back home or why she was so far away. It did, however, provide momentary comfort. For that, she was grateful.

They ate in silence for a while, until Marina asked, "So, where exactly are we?"

Taylah said, "This is Minnaburra, pretty much the only town within coo-ee."

"I'm not sure what that means," Marina tried to keep up, "You're talking too fast for me."

Cooper explained. "This town right here is called Minnaburra, and we're four hundred clicks that way," he held his left arm and pointed, "From Sydney."

"Clicks is a kilometer," Taylah translated.

Marina shrugged and made a nervous smile, "How much is that in miles?"

Now Taylah shrugged. "Dunno. But it's a four-hour drive. Five if the cops are clogging the roads with booze busses."

"Are you making fun of me?" They had to be speaking some kind of special language. *Is there an app for that?*

A rumble of laughter came from Cooper. A warm sound with lashings of confidence and a hint of dirty.

Dang he's cute. And his eyes are kind of multi-colored

mix of browns. Oops, better stop staring. "I will pay you back as soon as I get hold of my accounts again. I absolutely promise."

"No rush," he said with a slow blink.

Were they flirting? Their spoken language might be all over the place, but body language had to be universal, and he spoke it fluently.

A shadow came over their table. It was Pearl, standing right there in the cafe. How had she managed that?

Cooper grabbed the phone off the table.

Taylah yelped in shock as she turned to Pearl. "Cooper been giving you tracking lessons?"

Cooper shook his head, "Tay, don't."

Pearl nodded to the three of them and said, "Miss Beatrice sent me to find you and bring you home."

Taylah said, "We're fine right here."

"Seriously, please," Pearl looked panicked, then noticed their food, "Oh chips! May I?"

"Seagull." Taylah pushed her plate towards Pearl.

"What's for dinner back at the ranch?" Marina asked, as Pearl slid in beside Cooper.

Taylah giggled. "She said 'Ranch'."

"Probably lamb and potatoes again," Pearl said with a heavy sigh as she slid down.

"Lamb can be good," Marina tried to salvage the situation. Plus, if they got Pearl talking, it would delay their return to Boomerang. The pie was so filling, she wasn't sure she'd even need dinner at this rate. Whenever dinner was in this place, where the afternoons lasted forever.

"It's not lamb, it's two-tooth," Cooper said.

"It's what now?" She hated sounding like a broken record, constantly asking people to repeat themselves.

"Too old for lamb, too young to be mutton," Cooper obliged. "And I guess their first two teeth are in or something?" He finished with a shrug.

"Chewy as an old boot," Taylah added.

"It's quite hilarious," Pearl said as she finished the chips, "There we are sat around the table trying to act like ladies, while chewing hard leather. And then Miss Beatrice scolds us for being noisy eaters."

Taylah said, "Tell her you're veggo."

Marina raised her eyebrows in confusion, until she worked it out. "Vegetarian?"

"These Australians shorten everything," Pearl said. "Just to confuse people."

"You must have been here for a while, to understand them?" Marina asked.

"Nah," Taylah brayed out a laugh, "Just a steady diet of watching *Neighbours* and *Home and Away*."

The sight of Cooper checking his cell sent a pang of jealousy Marina's way. She wanted it in her hand, just for comfort's sake as much as anything. Cooper looked up, smiled and handed it over.

"I picked up on the really subtle vibe," he said.

"Not just a tracker, a psychic tracker," Taylah joked.

"Ease up, Tay."

In her charming British accent, Pearl said, "Quality banter."

Marina ignored the rest of the bizarre conversation as she checked social media again. Her account might be cut off, but she could still check the public feed and see if her name popped up. She might even be trending.

Huh?

Definitely not trending. Not even a little bit.

Why hadn't people noticed her absence for a whole day, possibly two with the length of the flight thrown in? Worry cramped her forehead. It was as if nobody cared that she'd disappeared off the face of the earth. Her parents on the other hand were making a huge impression, and a bad one at that.

Cooper pointed to a random place in the distance, "Look at that, a bucket of free chips!"

"Where?" Pearl turned to look.

"Quick, let's scarper while she's distracted!" Cooper said.

Taylah collapsed with laughter.

"I can't believe I fell for that." Pearl slumped.

The way they teased each other like old friends sent a pang of homesickness through Marina. How were her friends back home handling this news? And why weren't they raising the alarm about her lack of updates on the socials? Hadn't they noticed?

The app stopped refreshing, despite Marina repeatedly tapping her finger down the screen. "It's not working."

Cooper took it back and looked it over. "I'm prolly out of data," he said with a shrug. "I'll have to get a recharge."

"Oh good," Pearl said. "Now that you're finished, we need to go back."

It wasn't as if Marina had any other options. Unless Cooper was willing to drive them the four or five hours to Sydney? She could visit the embassy – there had to be one – and get a new passport or something.

Pearl added, "You have to come back with me or Miss Beatrice will sack me."

Marina brightened. "She can kick us out then? Great! I'd love to go home."

"Not you, me. I'm not a resident. I'm staff. I have to sing for my supper, so to speak."

"Then why aren't you staying in staff quarters?" The moment the words were out, Marina cringed afresh. Their tiny shared room had to be staff quarters. It would explain why it was so ... snug.

Pearl said, "Your accommodation is paid for. Mine's not."

"OK, data's back," Cooper announced. "Was just a drop out. There's still plenty on there."

They sat in the booth and ordered more chips, which Pearl ate like a model coming off zero carbs. Marina searched more social media feeds. Unable to get into her account with her millions of followers, she created a new one using Cooper's number, took a selfie and tweeted, "I'm in #Australia! Best food ever!" She also attached her old account name to the post, to help things along.

She needed her followers to find her and start talking about her again.

Perhaps a hashtag might help. #MissingMarina-Shenko should do it. That's when she noticed something getting a few more mentions – the family surname. Her food would make a reappearance if she wasn't careful. Yet she kept reading.

Randoms were hoping the whole family went to jail.

Not a single friend stuck up for them.

It burned Marina's gut not to be able to offer her parents comfort right now as they sorted out this hideous mistake. It had to be a mistake, right?

The moment she got home, she'd do everything she could to clear things up.

Odd that nobody was wondering where she was though.

And as much as creating a new account meant she could post, it also meant she had zero followers. Starting from scratch? Seriously depressing.

She cheered herself up with another selfie and a nod to Cooper.

The locals are gorgeous and super helpful.

That gorgeous and super helpful local who had given her a lifeline back to her people. He sure was a keeper. He seemed like good fun. She was sure she'd still like Cooper even after she got access to her money and bought herself a new cell.

A quick last message:

My Lovvies: sketchy wifi and data here, might be offline for a little while.

Don't do anything too crazy, K?

No replies at all. So, this is what they called 'shouting into the void'.

It physically hurt to hand the phone back. Real pain, making her neck tight.

With a smooth pull, Cooper tugged it away from her and put it in his pocket.

Marina's lungs weren't working. "I need some air."

"Yep. Time to go," Cooper agreed.

Together they made their way outside, into a blast of cool wind.

It was so hot just a little while ago. Marina shivered, noting the sun heading towards the ground way over in the ... she guessed it had to be the west.

"Gets a bit nippy at night." Cooper said.

The sky on the opposite horizon blazed dark blue. She jammed her hands in her pockets and tried to work out which way to go. Basic decisions like left or right taxed her brain as her breaths came fast and flurried.

Cooper took his jacket off and put it over her shoulders, pulling her in close.

"Doesn't take him long, ay?" Taylah said to nobody in particular.

Cooper said. "Ute's this way."

"I like the cold," Marina's teeth chattered as she

sucked in a cool breath. "I think I need it. Let me sit for a minute."

"OK." Cooper directed them to a bench seat near the car park and swiped the dust away. "But you'll have to keep me warm then."

He sat himself down, then placed Marina across his lap and held her closely.

"Oh, you're smooth," she said.

"Yeah-nah, I'm cold." He snuggled her in closer. "But I'm starting to think you're gunna be trouble."

***

Cooper didn't think he was high maintenance, but if someone wanted you to stay out in the cold with them, the least they could do was keep you warm. Especially considering he'd handed over his jacket.

Dead set, Miss Betty would have an epi when he got the girls home. But her high and mighty attitude was just an act. Trouble was, if he called her on it, she'd call him out too. So here they were, stalemate. Still, there were worse situations to be in.

They should have stayed inside, even if Pearl the Pom seagulled all their chips.

Marina wrapped her arms around him. "I'm sorry that I'm using you, y'know, as a distraction," she said. "Because I am going to go mad at that place. I can't call my friends, they don't know where I am."

"Yer olds really pulled one on you, yeah?"

She squinted at him in the darkness. "I'm sure that will make more sense when I'm not jetlagged. I only got here this morning. Or this afternoon. I don't even know what time it is because I don't have a watch. I mean, I guess it's night time now, because it's getting dark. Oh wow, these stars are amazing! Do you think you could give me your cell back, just for a little while?"

This girl was having serious withdrawal symptoms. "Did you do something *really* bad?" Wouldn't be the first.

Marina made a scoffing noise. "You'd think I'd run over The President. Which I didn't, by the way."

"That'd make you a hero."

"Pardon?"

"Kidding. Maybe your parents are spies and you know too much?"

"Ha! They are too boring to be spies. It's all art, art, art, art, and just to shake things up, more art." She yawned.

Not that he was bragging, but he found himself saying, "I know a thing or two about art."

"Probably not the same high-end stuff my parents are involved with," she said.

"Snob." What would she know?

"Wha –" An enormous yawn cut her off. So big he could see all the way to her back teeth. Then she did the most bizarre thing. She fell asleep.

Her weight sagged over him. He had to grab her to

stop her falling onto the ground in a crumple of zero dignity.

"Over here, little help?" Cooper called out to Pearl and Taylah.

Taylah grinned. "How are you two lovebirds settling in?"

"She's passed out."

"Oh my God, you didn't slip her a roh-ey didja?"

Panic wobbled his voice at the accusation. "No! She just flaked out all of a sudden."

Cooper maneuvered Marina into Pearl and Taylah's arms.

"She's famous, isn't she?" Pearl asked. "I mean, I know her name, obviously. But she's one of those people who's is famous just for being famous."

Taylah answered, "She's a NoozPoster, if that's the word you're looking for?"

"Oh yes, I've heard of them."

Cooper interrupted, "Who d'ya think she's hiding from?"

"I bet it's a mad stalker," Taylah said. "That must be why all her accounts are switched off."

Pearl said, "Being anonymous would be wonderful."

"Sounds like you know a bit about that?" Taylah shot back.

Pearl gave no reply until they arrived at Cooper's parked tray truck. Pearl had parked Miss B's rust-bucket station wagon next to it.

"I'll go in the tray," Taylah offered.

Pearl's jaw dropped. "Is that even legal?"

"Don't care."

Cooper was having none of it. "I can't lose any more points, so no-one's going in the tray. Pearl, help me get Marina in the back of yours."

Taylah helped too, and the three girls drove back to Boomerang.

Cooper watched the tail lights vanish in the distance as he got into his truck. He wanted to call on Marina again, when she was alert, not at the mercy of jetlag. He really wanted to find out what terrible thing she'd done to be punished like this. Wouldn't be the first time people had used Australia as their dumping ground for unwanteds.

Back at Boomerang, the girls were waiting for him to help carry Marina into the homestead. Marina was absolutely zonked and barely made a sound as they carried her in and lay her on a couch.

He asked, "What's the best time for me to come 'round tomorrow?"

"We can't have visitors," Pearl said. "It's not allowed."

Yet he also worked there. "Can't help it if our paths cross, but."

"Give her a few days, until she's not so fatigued." Pearl said.

Fatigued. It sounded so Pommy he wanted to laugh out loud.

Pearl gave him a sideways nudge towards the door.

"You need to leave now, please. If we break the rules we'll be in trouble."

Cooper snorted.

Pearl shout-whispered, "And keep quiet!" Then she bustled him out the door and closed it behind him.

Leaving him out in the cold.

Aches twisted Marina's muscles as she woke on a narrow . . . something. She guessed it was a couch. It couldn't possibly be a bed. Far too hard. And no pillows. She was still in her clothes and shoes from last night; her legs cramped and crumpled. Dry mouth with savory overtones reminded her of something she'd eaten. That's right, the little shop with stew pastries. And the cute guy. A smile formed as she remembered him. Then her tummy dropped as she recalled how many times she'd failed to access her bank accounts. Followed soon after by roiling nausea at the news items about her parents being raided.

Orange morning light danced through the lace curtains. She rubbed her eyes open to have a better look around at this bizarre old house with its strange rules.

The list of rules probably included 'no sleeping on the furniture'.

The stairs, which hadn't made any discernible noise during the day, creaked on every step. Of course, they did. The door to her room did not, which meant at least she wouldn't wake Pearl.

Too tired to find her pajamas, she slipped her shoes off and crawled fully clothed into bed. The mattress creaked and squeaked.

Marina had barely rolled (noisily) onto her side when she heard Pearl sit up. Pearl's bed squeaked and groaned just as much.

That noise was going to get old real quick.

"It's only me, you can go back to sleep," Marina reassured her.

Pearl made her bed. "I have to be up for shift."

"Mmmpf?" Marina felt herself drifting off. "What shift?"

"I'm on the morning roster to start breakfast."

"Wha' time isssit?"

"It's only five. Stay in bed, you're not due for breakfast until six thirty."

Six thirty? Who knew there was a morning version of that time.

***

Pearl roused Marina. Light poured in from the window, getting under her eyelids. "I'm not hungry," Marina muffled into her pillow as she rolled over.

Something skittered on the windowpane, giving it a good rattle but not breaking it.

"Your boyfriend is out there throwing stones at the

window," Pearl said, then added a giggle. "I think he'd like some attention."

Marina opened one eye out of curiosity. Seriously, was he throwing stones at the window? That's something her parents would have done, back in the old days before people had cell phones. Which only served to remind Marina of her miserable circumstances.

Pock!

"He is rather insistent," Pearl said. "It looks as if he has something for you."

"Kay-kay, hang on." With creaks and groans from the springs, Marina slumped out of bed. Then she pulled on a dressing gown over her clothes. Not because she was cold, but because she didn't want Cooper to see her in the same outfit as last night.

"What time is it?"

"Nearly midday. Luncheon is at one." Pearl said. "You missed breakfast and morning tea, by the way."

"Where's the kitchen, I'll get a salad or something."

"We're not allowed in the kitchen unless we're having cookery classes or preparing meals for others."

Of course. The rules.

Marina shuffled between the beds and cranked the pane open. "Hello there Cooper the distraction."

"She wakes!" He said with a grin.

It was a happy grin, not too smug. It went well with his sun-kissed cheeks from being outside in this heat.

"I brought you something. Ready to catch?"

Marina nodded, took a step back and Cooper threw

the small box straight through the open window. It sailed in and landed right on her chest.

"Oh my gosh, you got me a cellphone!" Marina leaned out the window and blew him a kiss. "You're wonderful! Thank you so much!"

"No biggie. Now we can text instead of me throwing stones atya window."

"You bet!" Marina said as she closed the window. A cellphone! Hands shaking with excitement, she pulled it out of the box and turned it on. Three out of five bars of connection. Wow! Connection! Maybe this tiny bedroom above the stairs had its advantages after all.

Cooper had already taken a selfie and put himself on the launch page. Cute. She opened the contacts list and found Cooper's number pre-installed. Definitely testing positive for confidence, that one.

"If Miss Beatrice finds out about that phone, she'll confiscate it." Pearl warned.

"Then she's not going to find out about it, is she?"

Pearl swallowed and said, "I guess not."

Marina doused herself in perfume and changed clothes. She'd packed for winter, so her summer options were severely limited. Only now did she realize how many days she'd been in these same clothes. The plane, yesterday, then she'd slept in them overnight. Urgh! OK, time to clean up. "Where's the shower?"

"Down the end of the hall, the bathrooms are on the right."

Marina grabbed a pair of clean jeans and her lightest top.

"You need to make your bed before you leave your room," Pearl called out. "It's one of t–"

"Rules? Yeah." Marina pulled the covers up and gave the bed a quick smooth-down with her palm, then made for the stairs.

A warm shower later, Marina dressed and put her hair in a messy not-quite-dry bun at the base of her neck. Slipping the phone and charger in her pocket, she headed downstairs, looking for any place she could suck some juice out of the wall.

"Marina! There you are." Pearl appeared out of nowhere. How did she do that?

"Quick, get in the library, they're all waiting."

No chance of finding a socket then.

In the library, instead of a communal guilt session, Miss Beatrice was praising the virtues of excellent posture. "One does not walk into a room, one glides in. Today, ladies, we shall be learning good posture by the tried and true remedy of balancing books on our heads. This discipline will correct your posture and improve your general deportment. One at a time please ladies."

Wait, *what*? This place was a brat camp, not a finishing school.

Bless her heart, Miss Beatrice really did put a hardcover book on each of their heads, Marina and Pearl included.

"Straight line, ladies. Heads up. Not quite so high Pearl, chin in. Glide, glide." Miss Beatrice said.

Clunk, thump, thonk, bompf. One after another the books fell off.

"It can't be done." Taylah said.

Prithee said, "This will take a while."

"Early days yet," Miss Beatrice said. "It matters not if the books fall, it only matters that you persevere until you are proficient. Once you are proficient, then you can aim for perfection."

Marina's mind whirled amidst Miss Beatrice's instructions and the sound of books hitting the floor. Her parents had deliberately sent her to the other side of the world; to protect her, or to get her out of the way. With her accounts closed and her social media profiles pushing daisies, her gut kept telling her it had to be the latter.

Step, step, wobble, step . . .

Perhaps this was the safest place for her to be?

The book slipped off her head again and landed with a thud. She hadn't even made one lap of the library. Oh well, back to the start.

Taylah said, "Look at me I'm doing it!" *Bomp.* "Bugger! I *was* doing it."

"Ladies, allow me to demonstrate." Miss Beatrice stood with her shoulders back and balanced the book between the top of her head and her chignon.

Marina scoffed. "That's cheating, your hairdo is doing half the work."

"Not in the slightest." Miss Beatrice lifted the book

away with one hand, pulled the pin and shook her hair out. Then she replaced the book and continued walking up and down, turning carefully but not unnaturally slowly, then walking back.

There had to be a trick to it. Marina tried again, but the dust jacket was so shiny the book slid onto the floor. Reaching for it, she got a closer glimpse at the tattered edges of the floor runner. The carpet would have been glorious when it was new, but that must have been a few decades ago.

Straightening herself, Marina folded the dust jacket away and placed it on a side table. The cloth-bound book had better grip. Rebalancing, she took careful steps forward. The book wobbled but didn't fall. Success!

Pearl and the other residents copied her, taking their slippery dust jackets off their books.

A few more laps of the room with the book on her head increased Marina's confidence. Others too were getting the knack. Pearl's smile became ridiculously wide, revealing large creamy teeth with a slightly crooked one on the side. So cute!

Pearl stacked a second book onto the first.

Other residents were doing the same. Prithee, in a colorful salwar kameez, already had four books on her head. Show off!

"The trick is to not concern yourself with anyone else." Miss Beatrice said. "Focus on your posture, focus on steady breathing and even steps."

How utterly crazy. The last time they'd been in the

library, they were talking about anti-social behavior in group therapy. Today they were . . . Marina wasn't exactly sure, but it felt like they were having fun!

The moment Marina's thoughts drifted back to her parents' situation, the books – two of them this time – biffed onto her shoulder and then the floor. She'd be covered in bruises by the end of this. Nobody else was stopping though, so she kept on trying.

"Chins in, ladies, we are not horses leaping over the gate." Miss Beatrice instructed.

Turning to complete a circuit of the room, Marina checked out the gorgeous portrait hanging on the wall. It looked like a glamour shot from old Hollywood, the classic colorized-even-though-it's-black-and-white look.

"Who's the hottie in the frame?" Marina asked.

Miss Beatrice said, "That is my beloved grand-mother, Hilda Zehren."

"She was a total babe."

Giggles filled the library.

"She was an astute businesswoman who guided Boomerang Estate thought the changing times of the 1940s."

Didn't seem like much had changed since then, though. Walking up and down a library with books on your heads was hardly an in-demand skill for NoozTu-bers though.

Marina's gaze kept roving to Prithee. She looked so interesting and different. The salwar kameez had the most gorgeous, intricate stitching in what looked like gold thread. Might even be real gold?

"Ladies, that is enough for now," Miss Beatrice said. "Rest and change for lunch, which will be served in the dining room."

Marina was all about fashion and frocking up, but why did they have to change for a meal? How formal was this going to get? Has she missed the memo about the theme for the day? This was so different from the day she'd arrived.

Then again, she wasn't as jetlagged, so maybe the other day hadn't been so ghastly and it had all been in Marina's head?

The residents placed their books into an empty shelf and began filing out. Miss Pearl remained and reached for the dust jackets, to wrap them back onto their correct books. A pang of guilt shot through Marina. She'd been the one to start the trend of removing the dust jackets, she'd better help tidy up.

"I'll give you a hand." Marina sidled up to Pearl.

"As long as you're not late for luncheon," Miss Beatrice said as she swept from the room.

Marina grabbed a spare dust jacket. The title was written in French, which upped the difficulty of finding its partner. It felt like visiting *BigBårn*, with all the display shelves filled with Nordic books.

She grabbed a title off the shelf but it had nothing printed on the binding or cover. She flicked it open to find the title page and squealed, "It's a dirty book!"

"A what?" Pearl jumped.

"Look at this!" Marina flicked through the pages. The text may have been in another language, but the pictures on the other hand needed no translation.

"Oh, my life!" Pearl said, trying to keep her snorting laughter down in case it brought Beatrice back in. "They're really going for it!"

"Wow!" Marina said, tilting her head at a particularly acrobatic illustration.

"I wonder if there's more?" Pearl grabbed another book off the shelf and opened it at a random page. "Oh yes. Lots more."

"Something tells me none of these jackets are not going to match."

"Got that right," Pearl grabbed a random dust jacket and slapped it over a book, then shoved it on the shelf. It was obvious the jackets were all fake, designed to obscure the true contents of the pages beneath.

"You're blushing!" Marina said.

"They're so lewd!" Pearl said.

Marina barked out a laugh. "I love your accent so much!"

"What accent?" Pearl said, then joined in the giggle. "These must have been well-mucky back in the day?"

Marina would never stop boggling at the Brit's strange expressions. Grabbing another book, she asked. "Do you think B knows about these?"

"I can't imagine she'd knowingly train our posture and walking style with these on our heads."

"Wait a moment." Marina checked the earlier pages to look for the publication year. "This one says nineteen thirty-five. Look how many reprints!"

Footsteps sounded in the hall. Marina and Pearl slapped the remaining dust jackets on and hurried up.

"Ladies," Miss Beatrice paused in the doorway, "Please be in the dining room presently."

Marina clamped her teeth shut to keep the giggles away.

"We'll be down now, in a minute," Pearl said.

"What a curious expression," Miss Beatrice said. "Do you mean now, or in a minute?"

"As soon as possible," Pearl clarified.

"Very well," Miss Beatrice turned and her footsteps faded away.

"Phew!" Marina let out a huge breath.

"We have nothing to worry about," Pearl said, "They're *her* books."

As they left, Marina paused to look again at the portrait of Beatrice's grandmother.

Pearl nudged her. "I think we accidentally found Granny's secret stash."

A giggle slipped out. "No wonder she's got a smile on her face."

Marina's bottom vibrated silently. Somebody was calling the phone in her back pocket.

Cooper!

Brilliant.

She shot out of the library and grabbed a sun hat from the stand near the front door.

"Miss Marina, where are you absconding to?" Miss Beatrice appeared just as Marina had her hand on the doorknob.

"I'm going out to lunch." Perfect timing, her stomach rumbled.

"Then you must sign the book for departures and arrivals."

So, they could leave if they wanted to? Things were definitely looking up. Marina picked up the pen, then nearly reached into her back pocket for her phone, stopping herself just in time. "Sorry, must still be jetlagged. What's the date today?"

Miss Beatrice told her.

"And the time too?"

Miss Beatrice pointed to an old-style clock on the wall above them. "You also need to write in your return time, so we will know when you're expected." Miss Beatrice added.

"Or you could give me my cell back and I can text you," Marina said as she wrote in her estimated return of four pm.

"Sarcasm does not become you," Miss Beatrice said.

Sunshine bounced off the dusty ground as Marina stepped outside. The air hissed with dry heat.

Cooper stood there waiting on the front porch wearing a friendly grin that was all kinds of adorable.

Keeping her voice low, Marina said, "Thank you very

much for the cell." Before she could stop herself, she planted a kiss on his mouth. Something zinged through her at the contact. The contact of his warm lips on hers fuzzed her brain. At least one thing in this living nightmare of outback brat camp was going right.

***

Busting a girl out of juvie? No biggie. The kiss? Unexpected, yet very welcome.

When Marina pulled back, her eyes were kind of hazy. "Let's blow this joint."

"You bet," came out on a gush of breath. He hoped it sounded neutral, while his heart did something weird.

She tucked her arm into his and nestled in close.

Nice!

There was something about Marina that made his system dance. OK yes, he'd checked socials and found out a little more about her. Not stalking. Just making sure her story – which he already ninety-nine per cent believed – checked out. And it did.

"Sorry about flaking on you last night. Jetlag sucks! I feel far more human today. And I'm so hungry right now my stomach is eating itself."

He grinned, "Righto."

"I will pay you back for the phone. I'm not a freeloader. As soon as I get access to my stuff again."

"You can take me out to dinner." *Did I say that? It came out sleazy.*

She laughed unselfconsciously, then playfully slapped him on the arm. "You're so funny."

Is that a good thing?

The moment the girl sat down in the cabin, she started tapping on her phone. It impressed Cooper that she could read in a moving car without spewing.

"What? Oh, come on!" She yelled out.

"We drive on the left here."

"No, not you, sorry. I still can't get into any of my bank accounts. Why would they do this?"

"Maybe it's not your parents. Maybe the police have shut it all down?"

"Why would they do that? I've done nothing wrong!"

"They must think you've done something."

"Victim blaming much?"

Yeesh. Things became incredibly tense and quiet for a while until he pulled up outside the cafe where they'd had pies yesterday.

She reached her hand out for his. "I'm so sorry. I'm normally a much nicer person than this. Truly. It's just that I'm so freaked out by everything going on."

"It's OK." Actually, it wasn't really, but he couldn't think of what to say, and he was starting to think they should get take away instead of eating in.

Her face was glued to her screen.

"You're so cute, I love your Throwback Thursday. Look how curly your hair was!"

"What?"

She held the screen up, he saw a photo he'd posted of

himself as a toddler. Heat roared up his neck and he shook his head. She'd found his Instafeed.

"Don't be embarrassed, I think you're adorable." She said.

***

Slow down girlfriend, you're coming on too strong. Marina scrolled through Cooper's socials they sat in the café and waited for their meal. *So, he bought you a cellphone? And pastries. That's no reason to go cray-cray. Although he is seriously cute. And he's trying to help, so you have to give him credit for that. She was itching to ask him what his family background was.*

Marina landed on a picture of Cooper from a few years back. He was standing between two adults wearing outdated pantsuits. She turned the phone around so he could see it. "Are you sure your parents aren't spies? They look like total spooks in this."

"That was . . . at a wedding in Sydney."

"In the seventies?"

Cooper chuckled. It sounded warm and throaty with that hint of dirty again. *Damn.*

"There was a certain *theme* to the day."

"Spies from the cold war era?" Marina said with a giggle that came out too sharp. She reined it in, hating that it sounded too loud. Why couldn't she have an elegant, *little* laugh?

"If they were Cold War spies, they'd at least be interesting. They're both boring old lawyers."

"Lawyers? Oh wow, good for them."

"Really?"

"Yeah, good on them."

"Okayyyy. That's not the response I usually get."

"Well, I think it's great." Uh oh, "I hope that didn't come out as patronizing."

"Why would it be patronizing?"

"You know, getting a college education, having a professional career. That sort of thing."

He gave her an unreadable look and shook his head. "You're weird."

"I'll take that as a compliment. And I'm impressed you know what The Cold War was. I mean, I know what it was because Daddy was a teenager in Russia in the 80s. He made it to the States in 1990, and a year later the old Soviet Union fell to bits. He likes to claim he laid the ground work for that."

Cooper gave her a blank look. She returned to scrolling through his pictures. "Oh my gosh, you have a carnation in your lapel and your hair is parted in the middle." *Seriously, themed weddings?*

"There was an open bar, it wasn't such a bad wedding."

Marina waggled her finger at him. "Tut-tut, underage drinking, naughty Cooper."

"I wasn't under age. We can drink at eighteen here," he said.

"Wow." Marina couldn't get her brain around that one. In the States the rules were twenty-one, and that was ages away. Hang on, did that mean Cooper was already eighteen?

Then again, even the limit of eighteen was a while away for her. "Your parents look really cool." Every nerve itched to ask more about them. For a start, they looked kind of white, but Cooper kind of *didn't*. Or maybe he tanned more in the sun? He did work outdoors a fair deal. Or maybe he was adopted? Did he have brothers and sisters or was he an only child? Was that getting too personal?

"So, you need to get to Sydney, yeah?" Cooper asked.

"Sydney would be great," Marina searched for an embassy or consulate. The website for American Citizens Services said she had to schedule an appointment online first, she couldn't simply turn up to reception. Something she wouldn't have known that if she hadn't had Cooper's phone. "When do you think we can get there? Maybe you could drop me off at a train station or something?"

"The train from Orange will take about five hours, if you get the express." Cooper said, "I'm heading down late next week for supplies if you can wait that long?"

The waitress came over with their plates of food and said, "Sorry for eavesdropping, but there's a fire just out of Bathurst that's gonna stuff you right up. Just thought you should know."

"It's like the world is conspiring to keep me here," Marina said.

"Good thing we've got plenty of pies then," the waitress said, leaving them to it.

"How big is this fire?" Marina asked, searching her phone for local news.

"It's not looking too great," Cooper said, sounding nonchalant.

That didn't sound so bad at first, but when Marina searched for an update, the images of sky-high flames freaked her right out. "You say 'Not looking too great' like it's no big deal, but that is an inferno from hell!"

And it looked like it would be burning for a very long time to come.

"Is there any other way we can get to Sydney?"

Cooper thought for a while. "We could go up to Dubbo, then across to Dunedoo –"

" –Now you're just making sounds!"

"Nah, these are real places!"

Marina got back onto her screen and searched for another consulate. "How about this place, it's Can-berra. Huh? They have their official big Ambassador's residence there. Cool. Let's see about a train to … oh what? It's going to be nearly ten hours on a coach! That's crazy!"

"Yeah nah, it's *Cann-bra* and you don't want that. I can prolly drive it in four."

"Then what are we waiting for? Let's go!"

"OK, we can do that, but doncha have to make an appointment first?"

"Oh yes, thanks! OK, let me just ... oh damn. They're saying I can only make appointments in Sydney. But they're so much closer in can-be ... I mean, *Cann-bra*. This is so unfair, why can't I go there?"

"Brutal," Cooper said.

"You said it!"

"In the mean time, you've got my sparkling company," he winked.

Marina burst out laughing. "My world has turned upside down, and here I am, sitting in a diner laughing my head off. Thank you for helping me see the funny side."

"Funny?" Cooper's face was utterly deadpan. "I was being deadly serious!"

For a second neither of them said anything, until they both burst out laughing.

Marina had no idea how this insane this new life of hers was going to turn out, but at least having Cooper by her side would stop her from going completely nuts.

Could her life become any more bizarre and confusing? If the celebrity news reports were true, Marina's parents were in all kinds of legal trouble back home. Frustration grew like a looming wave, ready to break over her. She should be home in New York, helping her parents. If only for emotional support. Yet here she was, on another continent.

But at least she had a phone. Thanks to Cooper.

"I have to get home," she said.

"But we haven't had any food."

"If I eat I'll throw up. I need my passport and I need to get home."

"I don't think that's such a great idea."

"I need to do something!"

"Yeah nah. I'll grab the pies and drive you back to Betty's."

D elicious aromas lured Marina and Pearl into the dining room, but they weren't allowed to eat yet.

Miss Beatrice said, "Now you're here. Luncheon will be served, once each place setting is completed in the correct manner."

Marina would starve then, as she studied the intricate place setting. If she'd had her phone, she could have taken a photograph. But no, this would be done the old fashioned way. Memorizing.

"Ladies, this is *service Parisian style*, tines and bowls down."

Marina looked around for the bowls but couldn't find any.

"She means the spoons are bowl-side down, " Pearl whispered.

Oh!

Today was getting seriously weird. It was as if they'd all suddenly transported to some fancy European finishing school, rather than a dusty old homestead in the outback.

Not even knowing what half the items were called, Marina picked up the little bone-shaped doo-dat and rested the fat-edged spatula knife over it. Pearl whispered that it was called a butter knife and the doggy bone looking thing was in fact a butter knife holder.

Of course it was.

Studying the table setting was an exercise in concentration and frustration, as her stomach rumbled. Her fault entirely for not being dressed in time for breakfast. But at least she'd made the book-balancing class.

And she knew something Miss Beatrice didn't. That might come in handy later on.

The setting required six different forks to the left of the plate, all in exacting positions, which Miss Beatrice checked with a flexible tape measure, just to be sure.

A narrow object above the plate intrigued Marina. "Is that a toothpick?"

"Heavens no, it's a nut pick," Pearl said. She shook her head and muttered something about Americans.

At another table, Prithee studiously completed her setting and stood back to check her work. This was Marina's chance to strike up a conversation.

"Wow, you're good. Have you done this before?"

The woman made a tilt of her head and said, "I researched before coming."

Which sounded like she wanted to be here, which ... how would Cooper say it? Yeah nah?

"Lucky you. I'm Marina, nice to meet you."

"I'm Prithee," she said with a shy smile. "Did you have time to research as well?"

"I didn't even know I'd be here until I got here."

"Oh goodness. Was it a surprise gift?"

Despite the fun they had this morning, this place was most definitely not a gift.

"It was definitely a surprise." Suddenly Marina

didn't want to say she'd been forcibly sent to digital detox. Not when the rest of the ladies here appeared to be so happy to snag a place. She softened it with, "My parents are hoping my stay will be beneficial."

"Mine too. I am very excited to learn all I can. Then I will be ready for my marriage."

Marriage? She didn't look any older than Marina.

"You're engaged?"

"Nothing so formal yet, but my parents are making inquiries. Do not be concerned, I will be meeting him first and will have veto if he will not suit."

"I didn't say anything." But the whole idea of arranged marriages felt so weird. "And you're OK with it, so that's what matters, right?"

"I know this will work. I trust my parents implicitly."

Well, that's something Marina didn't have. If she and her parents had more trust in each other, she would be at home in New York, helping them through whatever was going on, instead of being relegated to the sidelines and cut off from her people.

She managed a cheery, "Good for you," and studied the table setting even more intently, determined to ace this.

"Ladies, how are you coming along with your task?" Miss Beatrice came over with her measuring tape and checked Prithee's efforts. "Well done *Miss Pretty*, you have excelled yourself. You may help others now."

"I need help," Marina jumped in before anyone else

could claim her. "I can't get the glasses to look right." If she didn't get any help, she'd never get fed.

———

L ife settled in to something of a pattern over the next few days. Fun morning sessions that made Marina feel like she was in a finishing school, but serious sessions in the afternoon packed with group guilt and soul baring.

The whole time she still hadn't found a wall socket to charge up her phone. Watching the little phone battery symbol grow smaller and smaller sucked away at her will to live. Plus, she'd had no direct contact with her family since she'd arrived in Australia. Sure, she now had a phone, but she still had no money or passport, and no way of resurrecting her social media profiles.

Her life and career were officially over and she'd never felt more useless in her life.

She had, however, learned how to eat fruit with a knife and fork.

#LifeSkills.

The only thing that made the afternoon guilt sessions in the library bearable was the knowledge of the real content of the books on the shelves. Luckily Pearl came in with a tray of 'bikkies' and Marina accidentally made eye contact.

Eye contact that made her giggle.

"Is there something you wish to share, Miss Marina?"

"No, Miss Beatrice." Marina had to look away from Pearl or she'd fall about laughing.

"Tomorrow we shan't be having our sharing time. Instead, we are taking a day trip to an art gallery. I fully expect everyone to be on their best behaviour.

Oh wow, an art gallery. Brilliant! Something Marina could actually look forward to.

CHAPTER 6

Cooper drove the mini bus to the gallery for their 'artistic education'. Every resident of Boomerang Estate and Betty was on board. It felt weird to be the only bloke, but Betty didn't have the right kind of license to drive a twelve-seater, so he got the gig.

This way, he could also prove to Marina that he knew a bit about art. Not that he ever made a big deal about it, but he wasn't lying when he said he knew stuff. He just wasn't sure he knew how to turn his art history degree into a going concern. There wasn't exactly a shortage of gallery curators in this part of the world.

Arriving at the gallery, the residents and Miss Beatrice filed out of the bus. Lucky last, Marina walked out and Cooper's chest grew lighter. Two and a half hours of sitting and concentrating on the road was no big deal, but he also had to drive them back at the end of the day. And he wanted to walk around inside the gallery and check everything out.

Miss Beatrice gave instructions. "Now ladies, we are in public, that means we are representing Boomerang Estate and our families. Please be mindful of others. Master Cooper shall be our guide, so if you'd kindly guide us?"

'Master Cooper'? So denting for the ego.

Right then, he'd better lead from the front. He crooked his elbow towards Marina. She gifted him a smile as she wrapped her hand around his arm.

"Miss Marina, you shall walk beside me," Miss Beatrice said.

Coldness seeped into Cooper as Marina obeyed her teacher and reluctantly let go of him.

"Lead on, please, Master Cooper." Miss Beatrice said.

So he did. Through the streets, in public, feeling like his skin didn't fit the right way, because, how did he walk normally with a dozen-and-then-some women walking in pairs behind him?

For the entire walk, nobody even spoke. To him or each other.

That Miss B sure had them on a tight leash.

It may have been a small regional gallery, but there were some visiting masterpieces on national tour. It would be so easy to spend hours here with Marina, in the indoor air conditioned comfort, and forget the outside world for a while.

Vertical banners in the entry hall displayed the museum's visiting exhibition, a collection of impressionist works from the 20th Century. Marina's father had often dealt in works from that era, so she knew what she was in for. Vibrant colors with strong brushstrokes and movement. A departure from the realism as a result of the boom in photography that was taking off at the time.

The familiar style of paintings filled Marina's heart with worries about her parents. Of course, she'd brought her phone, and a charger. There would have to be a shop here, and they'd have to have a power socket, right?

Or, she could squash the worries right down to her toes and enjoy the outing with Cooper, even if she did have to share him with the rest of the residents.

Marina sidled up to Cooper and tucked her arm with his as she soaked up the atmosphere.

"You must know some good people here." She whispered as they reached the last few stairs.

He delivered that adorable grin. "My parents pulled some strings."

"Do they have an indigenous art section here?"

Cooper's eyes blinked rapidly. "Ahhh, dunno. Maybe? We could ask."

A few steps ahead of them, Miss Beatrice turned to cast Marina a stern look and shake of her head. After an exchange of confused looks, Marina pulled her arm away from Cooper's. Then Miss Beatrice smiled and turned back around.

Seriously? They weren't allowed to touch?

They weren't even allowed walk closely together, much less hold hands. Every time Marina drifted her fingers towards Cooper's, Miss Beatrice would magically turn around and give *that* look. The woman had radar!

And yet, there was something so utterly charming about sneaking glances at Cooper, and he to her. The way they touched fingertips on the sly as they rounded the corner. Or bumped shoulders as they walked through a doorway. The less they could touch, the more exciting each glancing brush became.

Their constant series of near misses became the highlight of the tour. Marina began plotting a reality television format where people on a date weren't allowed to touch at all. Ratings bonanza!

But also, they were in a gallery, and that always lifted her mood. So many wonderful artworks, from wall-hogging frescoes to modest portraits. There were more nudes than there were clothed portraits, but the style was so experimental Miss Beatrice didn't comment or rush them past. There wasn't anything to be embarrassed about, unless you had a dirty mind and looked *really* hard.

Cubists could be so helpful like that.

In a quiet corner, Marina took a seat. Her thumbs twitched to take selfies and share her day out. What was the point of visiting such a beautiful place if nobody else knew she was here? None of the residents were taking selfies. Instead, they stood for longer periods in front of the paintings, soaking up the details. It took longer to see each exhibit, instead of grabbing a snap and moving on. The benefit being the residents had to spread out much further, so they could all take turns absorbing the images.

There were school students here too, and at first Marina was so jealous they were using cell phones to follow a self-guided tour. Surely, Miss Beatrice could break the digital detox for educational purposes?

As the minutes ticked into hours, the group dispersed through the gallery, allowing Marina and Cooper to sit together on a bench seat.

He slipped his arm around her waist. "Missed you."

"I bet we'll get sprung any minute," Marina said as she rested her head on his shoulder. "This gallery is so relaxing. I would come here every day if I could."

Cooper suddenly pulled his arm away for no reason. Wait, there was a reason; Miss Beatrice walked in.

Miss Marina, "There is a Suzanne Valadon in the next room. Come along."

"Of course," Cooper said, rising and offering his hand to help Marina up.

Miss Beatrice gave *that* look again, so Marina stood up without touching him.

Cooper gestured his hand toward the next exhibit

and announced, "Mademoiselle Valadon was a self-taught impressionist, and was one of Renoir's models. She later carved her own career with both drawings and oil paintings."

Shock spread over Miss Beatrice's face. Marina grinned.

Cooper shrugged nonchalantly as they made their way into the Veladon display. "Told you I know stuff about art."

Instead of one or two paintings, they found themselves overwhelmed with artworks of and by Suzanne Valadon. In one Renoir, (it was only a print, not the real thing) Suzanne danced in a ruffled pink dress and floppy red hat.

There was also an enormous print of a famous Toulouse-Lautrec painting, called *The Hangover*.

"Must have inspired the movie," Marina joked.

Not a single laugh.

Tough crowd!

Marina strolled towards the next group of paintings by Suzanne Valadon herself, and suddenly stopped. "That's my Mom's!"

Everybody in the room turned to her, confusion galore.

She wasn't lying. The painting *was* her mother's. The vibrant colors of the *Young Girl In Front of a Window*, her gaze turned to the side as if there were something happening just outside the frame. Her arm resting casually around a jar of red and white camellias. Marina knew it instantly as her mother's work.

"You have a print of this at home?" Cooper asked.

"No . . . I mean my Mom–" Time slowed, her pulse bashed against her ears, her blood thickened.

Marina's eyes roved the artwork, from the ornate pedestal table to the lush greenery of the tree outside the window. The brushstrokes of the woman's blue and white dress which guided the viewer back to the the table again.

Marina slapped her hand over her mouth as she took in the signature. Suzanne Valadon, 1930.

She stopped breathing. Wanted to suck back all the words she'd said a moment ago.

Every pair of eyes fell on her as she swallowed past the boulder in her throat.

The truth stared at her.

She had seen her mother painting this very portrait. The exact same one. In the studio at home.

Marina had been watching from the balcony above the studio, as quiet as a long-held secret.

On the nights she couldn't sleep, she'd make a cozy nest out of pillows on the landing. The comfort of watching her mother painting in the studio below, lost in the mystery and magic of it all would send her to sleep.

This regional gallery with its perfect air conditioning was suddenly too stuffy and stultifying. She had to get out of here. Lungs so tight she may as well be breathing through a straw, Marina dragged in air with each painful breath.

"Is everything all right Marina?" Pearl asked.

Pulse thumping like a subwoofer in her ears, she searched for an exit.

"What's wrong?" That was Prithee, concern filling her face.

Marina pushed them away in her battle to get free.

White noise filled her head, as the pulsing, dragging, heavy burden of reality took hold.

A single thought beat like a drum.

My mother's a fraud.

My mother's a fraud.

My mother's a fraud.

Her isolation from home and exile from the internet.

My mother's a fraud.

Her parents not answering their phones. The ZMZ stories.

My mother's a fraud.

My mother's a fraud.

Her mother hadn't painted in the *style* of Suzanne Valadon, circa early 20th century. Her mother had pretended to *be* Suzanne Valadon.

And her father had sold those paintings as if they were Suzanne Valadon originals.

Fresh air promised relief as she found the emergency exit. The moment she pressed down on the door lever, alarms rang.

Not as loud as the alarms in her head.

My mother's a fraud.

My mother's a fraud.

The street outside was filled with warm air, ripe with summer. She gulped the life-giving oxygen.

She'd escaped the museum, but she couldn't escape the facts.

My mother's a fraud.

My mother's a fraud.

My mother's a fraud.

CHAPTER 7

The skull-scrapingly loud emergency alarm spread panic through the museum. Cooper's training kicked in. *Keep everyone calm (but don't say the word 'calm' as that creates panic) and tell them it's a drill. Then group people together and steadily guide visitors to the assembly area.*

But it wasn't a drill, he'd seen Marina push the emergency exit open, setting the alarm off. All the same, there were protocols to follow. Protocols which assumed one visitor might set off an alarm at one end of the museum to disguise a robbery in progress elsewhere.

And it would be really poor form if the gallery lost their exhibition because a girl lost her 'nana.

While performing a headcount of the Boomerang girls, Cooper calmly - there was that word again - checked for stray visitors who might be hanging back.

Surely their ears would be bleeding by now, as the klaxon broke through the pain threshold.

Right up until the panic attack, everything with Marina had been going so well. Sure, he'd been saddled with the job of driving them for the day, and driving them home, but he'd managed a few minutes of alone time. As 'alone' as he could be while guiding the tour group through centuries of culture, trying not to blush at the naked ladies and men on the walls.

Then Marina had suddenly begun hyperventilating, triggered by nothing more than a regular painting of a fully clothed woman sitting by a window.

The alarm clawed at his brain as he guided the last of the girls towards safety and bright sunshine outside. Cooper headed back into the building to make sure there were no lurkers. Although he wasn't officially on duty, he felt responsible for the disruption.

Thinking became impossible with the bone-splitting noise. He spotted a proper member of staff who gave the all-clear signal, and he was out of there. Taking the exit Marina had chosen - the alarm was already screeching, it could hardly get worse - he finally breathed once the door shut the noise off behind him.

Ears buzzing, he rubbed his head and steadied his breathing. He found Marina further down the lane. She looked like she was trying to merge with the weather boards of another building.

"What's wrong?"

Eyes jolting open, she looked ready to flee.

"Didn't mean to scare you." He really should work on his banter. But what was a guy supposed to say when his girl freaked out on him? Not that she was 'his girl' by any means. And maybe she never would be.

"Can't breathe," Marina clawed at the edge of her tee shirt. "Need air."

Then they should have stayed inside where it was cooler.

"Everything's OK. Do you want to go into the air con?"

"Not going back," she said between gulps of air.

A security guard came past, he must have seen them on the CCTV. "Is everything all right?"

"Not really. We were just–whoa!" He grabbed for Marina as she slumped, but her deadweight pulled him down with her. Their bodies crumpled on dry ground. What a disaster. Their first date ended with her fainting in his arms on the bench. Now this. Would the next date end up in the emergency ward?

Marina came around and blinked a few times, completely disoriented. "What the?"

"Are you all right miss?" The security guard asked as Marina made strange, half sentences and tried to get her bearings.

Disentangling himself from their pretzeled bodies, Cooper got to his feet, then helped Marina back to hers.

"Do you need medical attention?" The guard asked.

"No, no," Marina managed. "I'm so embarrassed. I just over-heated all of a sudden."

Which was a lie because it was temperature controlled inside. How did one 'over-heat' in air con? Marina's face turned from ash-white to flame-red faster than filling a wine glass. "This is so embarrassing. I've never passed out before."

"You're American?" The guard directed his comment to Marina. "Yeah, it gets pretty hot out here. Drink plenny of wahdah."

Cooper offered, "You're pro'ly dehydrated. I'll take you to the shop."

"I'll be fine, I'm so embarrassed," Marina said, smiling and blushing. "I'm so sorry. Please, I'm fine now."

The guard gave one of those, 'OK then, I guess you won't let me help you,' shrugs and walked back the way he'd come.

Cooper gave Marina a friendly hug and said, "Let's get out of here."

Fate wasn't on his side. Just as he thought they'd get some alone time, a determined voice said, "The young lady needs rest."

Miss Beatrice. Perfect timing.

She looked at Marina and said, "We should end our visit and return to Boomerang."

"But we barely got 'ere," Taylah said.

Miss Beatrice gave Taylah a look that wilted flowers. Cooper was glad he wasn't on the receiving end of that one.

He tried for a friendly tone and said, "I'll take Marina to the cafe and get her something to eat."

"I'm OK," she breathed.

She so wasn't. Neither was he. He'd seen people overcome with emotion from being in an art gallery, but he'd never seen anyone hyperventilate and freak out so fast. Except in the closing minutes of a really close league grand final, and that absolutely warranted it. Something very strange was going on here.

He didn't care if Miss Beatrice was watching, he put his arm around Marina's waist to hold her up. It felt right being there as they walked towards the caffeinated aromas of the gallery shop. "Let's get you a coldie," He could do with one as well.

"Excellent idea," Miss Beatrice said. "Ladies, we shall all move to the cafe. Remember your lessons. When we're in public, we are representing the school."

Teeth clamping in frustration, Cooper found himself walking at the head of a long line of young women as they walked to the museum cafe. It had to be part of Miss Beatrice's plan to not give them a moment alone.

"I'm so embarrassed," Marina said again as she took her seat.

"Stop saying that," Cooper gave her a wink and kept his voice low. "I'm getting drinks."

He came back with their sodas, and a chocolate chip cookie the size of her head. Then he took the seat closest to her and murmured, "Wanna to tell me how long you've been starving yourself?"

For a heartbeat she looked at him. Pure rabbit caught in the headlights. Then she shook her head. "Oh boy, have you got the wrong idea." Proving him wrong, Marina downed half her drink in two seconds, then attacked the cookie. She stopped only when there was a quarter of the cookie left. "Want some?"

Miss Beatrice hissed, "Miss Marina," from the neighboring table, as if manners were the most important thing in the world. They probably were, to her.

Cooper kept his voice low. "Do you have food issues? I have to ask, because you've passed out twice now and I can't help wondering why."

"S'okay," she finished the cookie.

Maybe she was pregnant? Didn't pregnant women pass out all the time or was that just in the movies? Maybe that's why her parents had dumped her in Australia? Because they were in the middle of some kind of investigation and a pregnant daughter tipped them over the edge? At which point things began to fall into place and he figured that painting she'd freaked out in front of had to have something to do with her parents.

Marina licked the crumbs from her finger. "I understand your concern and I thank you for it. I thank you for the sugar hit as well, because I needed it. I have fainted approximately zero times in my life before now, and then suddenly I have two in a month."

So, she admitted she'd fainted. That was a start. "Feel like sharing?" Would she be honest with him?

"I think, maybe, I had a panic attack," she said, looking at the ground.

With nothing else to go on, he'd take her word for it. For now.

Her voice moved back to regular conversation level and she sat up in her seat, shoulders back. "I apologize for flaking on you. Why don't we go take a walk outside and explore the town?"

The rapid change in subject gave him mental whiplash. Until, *Ahhhh, she must be saying this for the benefit of Miss Beatrice.* As he looked around the cafe, he noticed everyone had a juice or a soft drink - they couldn't all leave right now or they'd waste their drinks.

The girl was clever.

"There's still plenty to see here," Cooper said, hoping they could get lost amongst the exhibits. "I like the impressionists."

The color drained from her face faster than water from a tub. "I'd rather not."

Definitely the gallery putting her on edge. "Is it the paintings?"

She covered her face and said, "Can't we go outside again?"

"Can you be honest with me? Please?" He said as he led her towards one of the regular exits. He didn't want her using the emergency doors again. One noisy evacuation per day was plenty. "I won't tell anyone, I won't make fun of you, I just want to know what's going on."

She rubbed her face. "Fine, fine, it *was* the painting."

Outside, the late afternoon sunlight beamed like a lens flare in a JJ Abrams' movie. "Did the painting reminded you of your Mom or something?"

Despite the heat, her face turned paler than marble statues and her body shook. Cooper found himself saying, "Let me help you, please?"

She nodded and looked ready to cry. "You have to promise never to tell anyone."

"Of course," he rubbed her back as she gulped in cold air. "Don't be embarrassed about panic attacks. I used to get huge anxiety with spelling tests. Still can't spell to save my life."

Checking behind them to make sure nobody else was in earshot, Marina pulled him closer. "The reason I freaked out at the Valadon painting is because . . . I saw my mother . . . creating that *same* painting. I watched her paint it."

The pieces didn't quite fall into place though. "I'm missing something. You mean she painted in her style?"

"She painted as if she *were* the artist." Marina checked again to make sure there was nobody else around. Only CCTV, so she pulled him closer to make sure nobody would be able to lip-read either.

It was so hard not to kiss her right now, so close, he could smell the chocolate from the cookie on her breath.

"I only just realized when I saw the original Valadon. That's why I flipped out. I realized my mother is an art forger and my dad sells her fake paintings as if they're the real things."

"Oh my God!" Cooper's body buzzed with nerves. The entire concept was so alien it bounced against his brain and didn't want to go in. But it had to, because it explained everything.

Marina slapped her forehead in sudden realisation. "That's why she didn't like it when I watched her paint. When I was a kid. It wasn't that she didn't want an audience, she didn't want a *witness*."

The information finally penetrated Cooper's brain. Why Marina's family had abandoned her in Australia with no phone and no money. Or a passport to get home. "Holy crap, your Mom's an art forger?"

"Shush!"

Thinking became impossible over the white noise in Cooper's head. He pulled her into his arms and he kissed her hair. "This is some serious shit." No wonder she'd freaked out.

"Don't I know it!" came the muffled response against his chest. "I don't even know how to start unpacking all this crap."

"Your whole life they kept this from you?" he blurted.

Marina nodded and said nothing.

"Then go to the police and tell them you didn't know anything and you're off the hook, right?"

"Can I please just process this on an emotional level

before racing off into fix-it mode? Men never allow processing time, they just move straight into solutions."

"Yeah but, the longer you take, the more suss it will look."

"Stop talking, male-brain!"

Wow, talk about high-maintenance.

For the next few minutes, all Cooper could do was hold Marina and offer her comfort. It solved nothing, obviously. His mind filled with a word-salad of platitudes, and by some miracle he kept them to herself because he knew nothing he said could make it better. He kept on holding her, all the while thinking if they just went to the police and told them what they knew, or didn't know, Marina would be off the hook.

But she said she wanted processing time. Or whatever. And hey, the hug was good. Finally, something sensible formed in his head. "Who else knows you're here?"

"Just my parents, I think. And a couple of friends. I haven't been able to do much with the cell, I mean, mobile, since you gave it to me because I haven't been able to recharge it."

She wasn't thinking. She was reacting, and he needed her to be able to think clearly. Hmmm. Maybe she did need processing time. In order for things not to get any worse, using the mobile to reach out would probably be the wrong thing. Especially if everything was so public.

"I know you're stressed, but I need you to think

about your socials. You've said you're in Australia, but have you told anyone what part?"

"I don't think so."

"Did you tell your friends where you were?"

"Um . . . no. I didn't," Marina wiped her cheek and shook her head.

"Did you disable the settings on the location pin?"

That got her attention and she turned pale and scared again. "I don't know. I don't think I did."

"We need to disable that right now."

Shaking, she surrendered her cell, the one she kept tucked in her bra. Then she pushed back and took a deep breath. "I can't absorb this. I should be home with my family. But all I want to do is scream at them for lying to me for my entire life."

The dry wind picked up, baking Cooper's brain. "We should probably find some more shade so you can chill."

"You're so practical," Marina said as she turned towards the footpath. "I just want to crawl into a cave and never come out."

But they had the rest of the Boomerang residents he had to get home first, and that was a two-hour drive. "The front passenger seat on the bus reclines a bit, you can sleep on the way home."

"I don't think I can sleep this one off."

"Just pretend then."

"You're a keeper."

They took a few steps back to the gallery cafe when Marina pulled up short. "She knows who I am!"

"Who are we talking about now?"

"Pearl. She knows who I am. She could tell other people where to find me."

"Does Pearl have a mobile?"

"I don't think so."

"Then there's nothing to worry about. Keep walking."

"What if she uses one at the chalet? She's on staff, she must know where one is."

What she said wasn't all that logical, but it made sense in a way. In a scared, panicky, paranoid way. "I have a feeling that maybe Pearl and Miss Beatrice are on your side. I think they've been trying to protect you all this time. And as far as anyone else knows, you're just a bratty American on digital detox."

"I guess so. But they must recognize me?"

Spoken like someone who'd lived their entire life in the spotlight. "They might think they have, but you don't need to confirm it. I mean, I get mistaken for a Hemsworth all the time."

Marina laughed so sharply she snorted. Seriously, a Hemsworth? Props for cheering her up when everything else was turning to crap. Sneaking a sideways glance, she laughed nervously. "You're a sweetheart for cheering me up. Thank you." For a few seconds, they were just a couple of teenagers taking a walk. It almost felt normal.

"I can't imagine how stressful this is for you," Cooper said. "Let's keep walking and –" they stopped as Miss Beatrice, Pearl, Taylor, Prithee and the rest of the finishing school residents strolled around the corner.

Miss Beatrice stepped towards them. "There you are. I think it's time we return to Boomerang. If we stay much later we shall have more traffic to contend with."

If only Cooper didn't have to drive, he could spend the next hour or so deleting Marina's newly-madeaccounts and helping her disappear from the world again.

Marina pretended to sleep on the drive home. If she got lucky, she might even fall asleep for real. No such luck, her brain would not shut up.

That painting.

Her mother painting that same painting.

Stroke for stroke.

I mean, kudos for the insanely great skills, but holy guacamole, with such amazing talent, why didn't her mother just paint her own art? Her dad could have sold them for plenty of money.

The processing time really helped, as did the solo seat, so nobody could sit next to her and try to chat. She needed a clear head.

The clear head brought clear thoughts. Cooper was right. She needed to go to the police and tell them she didn't know about any of this. It would be difficult to convince them, but it had to be done. Hiding out only made her look guilty.

The only way to clear her name was to come clean, officially.

Once again, she reached for her phone, then stopped herself. Wow, what willpower! She'd need all the willpower in the world to endure the insanity to come. But if she posted anything, even privately to her friends, there was a risk she'd drag them down with her.

Impossible.

A drumbeat in her head as the coach chewed up the road.

My parents are frauds.

I must clear my name.

My parents are frauds.

I must clear my name.

Being her own worst enemy, she snuck a look at her new instafeed account. The followers were low. *Embarrassingly* low. Like, she'd actually have to start following other people and ask them follow back.

Amateur hour.

Which only brought home how fickle her real followers were, considering they weren't coming across to her new one.

How odd. A few days ago, that would have sent her

into a tailspin. Now she had so many bigger issues, this barely made a dent.

———

She was the last one out of the bus. Cooper came over to check she was OK.

"I don't think I can be."

"I'm sure everything will be OK. Just because the anxiety train has pulled in, doesn't mean you have to get on."

"That's a great visual. I'll remember that." Maybe she *could* hide out from the world. Maybe her parents had done her a favor after all and sent her somewhere safe. Well, at least isolated. And life here wasn't so awful. Sure, the afternoon group sessions sucked but the mornings were fun. It was almost as if the estate had a split personality. Finishing school in the morning, reform school in the afternoon. And once she got used to that, she'd be fine.

Ok that was a lie. She *never* would get used to it.

Cooper gave her a friendly squeeze. "This feeling will pass. Put it this way, when was the last time the news made you super-pissed? And how soon did that same thing become old news?

"Oh yeah." The image of a smiling 'promising athlete' who'd gotten off with little more than a slap on the wrist for a disgusting assault came mind.

"How long did the outrage last?"

"I know what you're getting at, it was over after a few days, right? Well, the one I'm thinking of lasted a fair while. It was like, two weeks or something. And then it started up again when he got out."

He hugged her closer. "And then what happened?"

"I don't know it just kind of," she rifled through the cluttered drawers of her memory, "It kind of vanished because there was that virus."

Miss Beatrice made a pantomime cough about their embrace, and he withdrew.

The cool afternoon wind took his place. So odd that the days were so hot and the nights were so cold.

"I know what you're trying to say," Marina felt sick even thinking it. "This will be really bad for a short while, then I'll be conflictedly grateful for a pandemic to take the heat off."

"I'm not saying you should pray for bad news. I'm just saying it won't last forever. It will go away."

"But this is the problem. My business model relies on me *not going away*. How do I make this go away without losing my social currency in the process? Because I really don't know how I'm going to recover from this."

He wrapped his arm around her shoulder again and drew her into his warmth.

"That's enough, Miss Marina," Miss Beatrice said. Even though it was Cooper doing all the snuggling.

They'd reached the chalet steps anyway, so she had to say goodbye to Cooper and go inside with everyone else.

Keeping her voice low, she asked, "How about we try for a dinner date?"

Miss Beatrice counted the residents as she guided them inside. "Miss Marina, there is to be no further fraternizing."

Cooper did that clumsy wink thing and said, "I'll chuck a stone at your window."

Instead of a warm kiss goodbye, she could only wave farewell.

Miss Beatrice cleared her throat again and waited by the door.

"What are you going to do? Expel me?" Marina marched past her, then took to the stairs. Honestly, why did she have to be so strict? Would one farewell kiss break the very fabric of space time?

"And where do you think you're going?"

"To my room."

***

She'd barely slipped her shoes off and slumped onto her bed than a knock came to the door. "It's only me," Pearl said as she came in.

"Not now. I don't want to talk." Which was strange because a few minutes earlier she'd been complaining about her lack of social media access. Face-to-face stuff was so much more confronting.

"I wanted to thank you for today, the gallery was stunning."

Was she deliberately not listening? "I don't mean to sound so blunt, but I really need some alone time right now."

Marina grabbed the pillow and shoved it over her face. The moment she closed her eyes, she was a child again, watching her mother paint from her secret spot on the landing. Not the image she wanted right now.

"I don't understand you, I really don't." Pearl said. "You complain because you're cut off from the world. Yet here I am, offering conversation and you cut me off and I merely–"

"–I can't even!" Marina threw the pillow onto the floor and sat up. She was still trying to absorb everything from today.

"Can't even what? Why do Americans never finish that sentence?"

Red mist falling over her eyes, Marina glared at Pearl. "I've had a really bad day, and it's got nothing to do with you. And I'm coming across as a total B and that's not me at all. And I don't want to start a fight, because you're a really nice person."

Red blotches spread over Pearl's beautifully white forehead. "But it was a wonderful day!"

"Not for me." Marina lay down again and curled into fetal position.

"You had plenty of opportunities to sneak off with Cooper. I deliberately kept Miss Beatrice occupied so you could have more time." Pearl huffed. "Oh please, stop thanking me, it's embarrassing."

Taylah tapped on the door and came in. "Just checking to see if you're all right?"

Another person in here? Marina begged, "I really need to be alone right now."

"Nah. Ya need a caddel sanwedge. C'mon Pearl, you take the left, ready, set, go!"

Before Marina could work out what Taylah was talking about, she found herself squished in a three-way hug and suddenly she understood. Cuddle sandwich.

Tears spritzed out of her eyes. She'd so very nearly shouted at them and demanded to be left alone. "Ohmygawsh you gyze. Thank you for ignoring me. I had no idea how much I needed this."

"Cures what ails ya," Taylah said.

Marina would work out what she'd said later. Right now, she luxuriated in the love bomb. "I've been so awful to you, and you're both being so nice and I'm so sorry. You must think I'm the biggest pain in the world."

Pearl said, "We recognized the stress you're under. You were upset at the gallery and we wanted to help, but you ran off and Miss Beatrice corralled us together."

"Yeah, but I managed to look you up and . . ." Taylah shrugged, "Your parents are dodgy brothers."

Slowly, Marina sat up again and hugged the pillow to herself. "I need to be able to trust someone with this right now. It's so overwhelming."

"You can trust us," Taylah said. "But you gotta promise not to tell anyone I'm here. My name isn't even Taylah. It's Tash. My boyfriend was caught importing pseudo and he's rolled over so I have to hide out until it's all sorted. Pearl here –"

"I can tell my own story. Taylor, or Tash, I guess I should call you,"

"Nah, still call me Taylah. Pro'ly for the best."

Pearl sighed and made her confession: "I'm running away from my parents, who were also my managers. They invested all my earnings and lost the lot. And the papps went into overdrive when I turned eighteen, like I was fair game. And then every offer I received required nudity and that wasn't going to happen. Things got so insane I had to get out. So yeah, I'm out here hiding rather than facing the mess. And I'm broke, so I'm working, except I don't have a working visa so please don't tell anyone or I'll get deported."

"She was a soap star," Taylah/Tash said. "I knew who she was straight away."

"Really?" Pearl asked. "You never said anything."

"Didn't wanna fangirl."

"Thanks for not blowing my cover."

"Thanks for not blowing mine," Taylah added.

Pearl and Taylah-Tash hugged each other and Marina had to laugh. "Is there anyone here at brat camp who is a genuine brat or are we all hiding out and pretending?

Pearl and Taylah laughed.

"Does Miss Beatrice know who you really are?"

Taylah shrugged. "Pro'ly not!"

Marina found herself laughing at the bizarre situation they were all in.

Pearl got up and made for the door. "I have to get back to work. See you at dinner?"

"I'm not hungry. But thanks anyway."

Taylah pulled a phone out of an inside pocket. "I know I look like a bogan wearing flannel, but men's clothes have so many more pockets."

"Yes, they do!" Marina giggled. "Hey if you stand by the window you can get a signal. How are you charging yours up, by the way? Where's the socket?"

"Kitchen. Behind the microwave."

"Of course!" Marina slapped her palm onto her forehead. "I am so lame."

"Too many people down there now, tho. We'll go in later when it's all quiet and suck some juice out of the wall."

"You've got this all worked out, haven't you?"

Taylah shrugged. "Not everything. What about you? What are you going to do about your parents and the art crimes?"

Art crime. That was a pretty blunt way to put it, but as Marina thought about it, well, that's what it was.

"I don't know what I'm going to do. Cooper says I should go to the police. Which is odd because, well, back home his folks would avoid the police like the plague. I'm still in the shock phase right now, I just want sympathy and hugs. I haven't reached the planning stage yet. I don't even know where to start."

"Well, you might want to start planning something soon because this is not looking good." Taylah held her phone out and showed Marina the screen. Her father was in custody, her mother under house arrest - presumably her brother was either in the house with Mom or staying with relatives. Who were probably under a fair amount of suspicion as well.

"They'll be coming for me next, won't they?"

"If they can find you."

"Being out of sight is kind of appealing right now."

"Yeah but if the media turn up here, you might blow my cover, and Pearl's.'

Oh shit. "So, if I contact the media to clear my name, I have to go to them, they can't come here. Otherwise you're screwed."

"Pretty much."

"Should I go to the police?"

"Not the local ones. You pro'ly need to head into Sydney so you talk to the right people who can get in touch with their equivalents in the States."

"Is there any media in Sydney I could talk to as well?"

Taylah paused for a beat then said, absolutely deadpan, "Yeah, we got a couple."

That night as Marina tried and failed to get to sleep, she checked her cell phone. In a few minutes, she'd sneak downstairs and use the socket behind the microwave. Once Taylah was finished. She desperately needed to call her friends and tell them what was going on. But she also couldn't tell anyone, so even if she swore her friends to secrecy, she'd be paranoid one of them would accidentally blurt it out.

The safest option was to say nothing and keep them out of it.

Yet she couldn't put the phone down.

Time to admit it was an addiction?

I can stop any time I like.

Marina pressed her thumb over the button to log herself in.

Huh? The phone shook. *Fingerprint not recognized.*

She tried three different angles but the phone still wouldn't open for her.

Damn thumb sweat.

She pressed in her code but the phone shook and told her it was incorrect. She tried again, but the same thing happened. This time it locked her out for the next five minutes.

Maybe it was the universe telling her to stop, even for five minutes. Time to see if she really was addicted.

I can wait out five minutes, no problem.

Five minutes took forever to arrive.

Frustrated, she shoved the phone under her pillow. *I*

don't need the phone, and anyway, leaving it alone will preserve the battery. I'll be fine, it's only one night anyway.

The more she lied to herself, the more she might come to believe it.

Taylah tapped on her door once, waited a beat, then once more. Their signal that the coast was clear. OK, at least she could charge the thing and start with a full battery tomorrow.

CHAPTER 8

For the first time in ages, Marina was up and dressed for breakfast. But they weren't eating any time soon.

Miss Beatrice stood in the middle of the dining room, holding a cellphone in her hand. "Nobody eats until the owner steps forward."

Marina completely lost her appetite. What an idiot she'd been. After Taylah helped her find a socket, she'd plugged in late last night and then . . . gone to bed and fallen asleep!

Miss Beatrice held the device aloft. The screen flashed on with a reminder.

10am shrink.

Wait, what? She had a shrink appointment?

Did they have counselors coming to the chalet as part of the digital detox program?

Then she mentally slapped herself. *This must be*

Cooper's phone! That was why her fingerprints and her pass code hadn't worked last night.

If she had Cooper's phone, he must have hers. No sooner had that thought crossed one side of her brain to the next, she raised her hand and made sure everyone would get breakfast that morning.

"It's mine. I'm so sorry. I know it was wrong, but I just couldn't help myself. I am addicted and I need to detox." She held her hand out to take it back and shut it off. Nobody else needed to see Cooper's appointment. "I'll turn it off and pack it away."

Shame she couldn't get into it and send herself a text - for Cooper to see - to arrange a phone swap. On the other hand, if he realized the switcheroo, maybe he could text himself a message with his code in it so she could open the . . . oh wait, she wouldn't be able to open the phone to get the message.

"This is confiscated." Miss Beatrice said. "Marina, you shall help Pearl in the kitchen."

For the next hour, Marina followed the bustling figure of Pearl as she set about quietly but quickly making place settings in the dining room.

"OK." Pearl blew imaginary hair out of her eyes. "How about you put the cereals and bowls on the serving table?"

"Yes, of course. Just tell me where the cereal is?"

"In the pantry."

"Good. And where are the –"

"– bowls are in the cupboard. Double doors, down the end."

"I'm on it."

Boxes were boxes, so all she could do was set them out in a neat row. Then she put the bowls at the head of the production line she'd made. She took it upon herself to fetch a stack of spoons from the drawers to place near the bowls. Showing initiative and all that.

Oh, and the milk too, she even thought of that. In the refrigerator she searched for the Half and Half. Instead, she found an enormous plastic bottle that boasted "*Three litres of full-cream milk*". Whatever that was.

It sure was heavy.

When Marina showed off her display to Pearl, the woman turned white. "Miss Beatrice will have a fit!" Pearl's mouth tightened so much her lips nearly disappeared. In a flurry she bustled everything off the table and returned it to the kitchen benches. A moment later she brought out a glass drink dispenser and decanted the milk into it. The woman blurred between the kitchen and the table again, bringing out large bowls, three-quarters full of cereal.

"Take these soup spoons back."

"I was only trying to help." Marina returned the cutlery and came back with dessert spoons instead.

"No, we don't need them, they're already on the table."

"Oh." Wow. She really sucked at this. Really, truly, absolutely sucked. Cold emptiness drained her energy away. She couldn't even prepare breakfast for house guests. Not completely her fault, she hardly ever had breakfast. Because she slept in. Or had coffee instead. Or picked up a muffin from the side table.

Muffins! There were no muffins. "I know how to make muffins!" She bragged. There had to be a muffin mix in the pantry somewhere. Hunting through the shelves revealed no cake, slice or muffin mixes. Just lots of tins with labels such as self-raising flour, baking powder, sugar, plain flour and corn flour. There was even an unopened bag of coconut meal.

"Can you get the eggs out?" Pearl came back in.

Eggs! She'd need them for the muffins anyway. What luck, there was a whole tray of eggs right on the shelf. Lifting them carefully, a thought popped into her head that this must be where the expression 'don't put all your eggs in the one basket' came from. None of the eggs cracked as she put them down. Phew! She did something right!

"I thought I'd make muffins," she announced.

"Please don't, we're already running behind."

A deflated balloon couldn't feel flatter. "Should I just get out of the way."

"That would be for the best."

If she'd had a tail, it would be tucked under like a dog's. Marina grabbed the phone from the wall and trudged back to her room.

"I suck at everything." The second the words came out, she had to admit they were true. Time to cancel the pity party of one, because that wouldn't achieve anything aside from self-imposed misery.

There had to be something.

Aside from being famous for making videos on YouTube. Which wasn't a complete waste of time. She excelled at social media and getting attention. It earned her a few thousand dollars a month in advertising and sponsorships. But that was when she'd had a good reputation. Before her parents had been exposed as frauds. Picking up where she left off would be impossible with such damaged credibility.

She rubbed warmth into her shins and tried to think what else she could do. Obviously, she'd have to deal with the tsunami of negativity heading her way, but once that was over – and at some point it had to be over, right? – what would she do with herself?

Absolutely nothing came to mind.

At least she could make muffins.

———

Everything smelled wonderful, and even more surprising, the muffins turned out perfectly (with Pearl's help) and she was starting to feel hungry. Maybe this breakfast thing could work for her? There was coffee and a spare seat next to Prithee. As the rest of the residents took their seats, Pearl and Miss Beatrice put plates of bananas and oranges in the middle of the tables.

Miss Beatrice announced, "Ladies. This morning we shall be learning how to eat fruit."

"Stick it in your mouth," Marina whispered to Prithee.

Prithee smiled but did not laugh out loud. Tough crowd.

Miss Beatrice continued her instructions. "You may be at a function where the fruit arrives with its skin intact. Or partially intact. Or the fruit may have seeds, pips or stones. This morning we will learn to handle any situation with grace and a minimum of fuss. If we sent the food back, or refused to eat it, it could upset our host. We don't ever want to upset our host, that is the very worst form of rudeness."

That statement felt purely for Marina's benefit.

"We will begin with whole fruit. An orange and a banana. As I said, it is unlikely you will ever be at a function where the fruit is presented in such an unprepared state. But on the condition that it is, you will have full confidence and the necessary skills to handle the situation with elegance. We begin with the orange. Everybody take an orange and put it on your plate, like so."

They all did.

"Now take your fruit knife."

Marina reached for a knife.

Mis Beatrice said, "No, Miss Marina, that is the butter knife."

She put it back, checked what Prithee had, then grabbed the same one from her setting.

"That's the one. Now ladies, hold the orange on your plate delicately with your other hand. We do not force it down into submission, we merely hold it steadily in place. Cut the ends off the orange, top and bottom, like so."

Miss Beatrice demonstrated the skill on her own plate. "Depending on the ripeness and cultivar of orange, there will be some juice. It's unavoidable, which is why we need to be delicate. We cut thin strips of the peel, not too deeply, from top to bottom, and place the peel on the side of the plate. Now you have your naked orange."

Pearl came over to sit beside Marina with her own fruit, joining in the class. As the general noise level rose from people chatting while they tried the technique, Prithee leaned over and said, "You are quick witted. I had to hold my breath so I wouldn't burst into laughter."

So, she had liked the joke. "Sometimes I can't help myself."

"You'll get us all into trouble I'm sure," Prithee said as she sliced the top off her orange.

Was that a criticism or an observation? *Concentrate,* Marina told herself, as she sliced the ends off her fruit as delicately as she could. Admittedly, she wasn't yet twenty, but in her whole life she'd never faced a situation where she needed to peel fruit with a knife and fork. Everything always came readily cut in little bite-sized pieces. That's what staff were for.

"Swift, sure motions are the best," Miss Beatrice told

the room. "Sitting there sawing back and forth for an eternity achieves little."

Peeling oranges hardly felt like a useful life skill. Then again, if she had her accounts back up, Marina could have periscoped the activity.

Dang. Everything always came back to social media.

"Now it's my turn to apologize to you," Pearl said under her breath. "I was short with you this morning. I'm sorry for causing offence. I'm so used to doing things myself, that's all."

Relief washed over Marina. "Can we start again tomorrow? I'll study the layout today and I'll be able to help you properly and set things out the right way."

"Why don't we see how you feel in the morning. Perhaps we'll rise a little earlier so there is more time to learn how to do it?"

Cold dread filled Marina at that thought.

Prithee leaned over, "I don't mean to interrupt, but I couldn't help overhear your discussion about breakfast. I was wondering if we could introduce some new items? Like string hoppers or sambal and maybe a dhal or fish curry?"

Pearl leaned in to mirror Prithee. "That would be brilliant. Breakfast curries are *well good.* Do you have a favorite recipe?"

They became deeply animated over the glories of curry for breakfast, as they plotted what they'd need to buy to make it happen.

Who the heck said things like 'well good' anyway?

Marina sliced at her orange, squirting a thin stream of juice across the white table cloth. Another cut of the orange, another small squirt of juice. It was embarrassing, but it also gave her an idea. She turned her knife around and cut the orange, squirting juice on herself.

"Miss Beatrice, I need to change my top."

The rest of them could keep cutting their fruit. Honestly, if she were at a party sometime in the future and the dessert came out like that, she'd pass. She grabbed a muffin and headed upstairs. She changed, then figured she'd have a quick lie down.

P earl roused her. "Your boyfriend is tossing stones against the window again."

"He is?" Wiping drool from her cheek, Marina said, "What time is it? I'm completely disoriented."

"It's nearly lunch. You've slept right through the fruit lesson."

Something skittered against the window.

She opened it.

"Good afternoon," Cooper beamed up at her.

"Hello. Oh! Before I forget, Miss B confiscated your phone. Well, she thought it was mine, but we must have mixed ours up at some point."

"Yeah, I've got yours. Here, catch!" He threw it up to her and she caught it.

"By the way, your phone beeped with a reminder

about a shrink appointment at ten. I'm sorry I didn't tell you earlier."

"Whatever," he shrugged.

"Mental health is important, I hope you went!" She said.

"Wanna say it a bit louder? They didn't hear you in Perth."

Why would someone be embarrassed about health? Must be some kind of Australian thing she hadn't worked out yet. The people here sure were weird.

Dust plumed in the distance.

There were cars approaching. No, not cars, these looked like SUVs, with some kind of appliances on the roof.

Cooper turned to look in the same direction, and swore obscenities.

The media had found them.

CHAPTER 9

Cooper and Marina bundled into his car and fled Boomerang Estate. If this were a proper road, they could have been a little more discrete. Alas, the plume of dust behind them gave their location away. It didn't take long for the media caravan to pick up the scent.

Marina's phone buzzed. "It's Sophie."

Cooper's forehead creased. "How did she get your number so fast?"

"I was messaging her the other day, remember?"

"That was a message, not a phone call." He took the turn towards the main road into town.

"Listen to you, detective Den Brave." Marina tapped the screen.

Cooper said, "Don't tell here where you are. Don't even say you're in Australia. Don't say anything about time zones."

"Cool it James Bond, it's just Sophie." Hitting the speaker button. "Hey Sophie, what's up?"

"*Oh my Godfather, things are going crazy here Ree, the feds are raiding our house right now!*"

"Why your place?"

"*Shit just got way too real. I can't even. What kind of shady deals were your parents involved in?*"

"I don't even know where to start." Not a lie.

"*Try me.*"

Cooper pulled over near a riverside reserve. He put his hand over the phone and shook his head, then he mouthed, "Call her back."

"*Ree? Are you with someone? Who's there with you?*"

"It's OK. I'm just having a hard time getting my head around everything that's happened too"

"Where are you honey, we're all worried about you. Lemme come pick you up and we'll get some frappachinos or something."

"I hate frappachinos," the words were out before Marina realized what her friend was trying to tell her. Sophie had just said there were federal agents in her house. They could be forcing her to make this call, listening in the whole time. Frappachino had to be code. Panicking, she quickly said, "My battery's about to die, I have to go."

"Switch it off," Cooper said.

"I have."

"No, switch it off-off. Hold the button down and power off."

Double-take. "I never do that."

"Well, you need to. The battery will last longer for one thing. And if it's switched off, the locator's not triangulating all over the place and giving you away." He checked the rear mirror. "I think we lost them."

"Fine, I'll do it." Bossy man. Also, "We lost them already? But we hardly took any turns?"

"Yeah, I know. Maybe they ... oh damn, maybe they have pulled in to the estate?"

"They'll blow Taylah's cover!"

The phone powered completely off. Now people couldn't call her, which, given the circumstances, might not be such a bad thing. It meant she'd have to wait for it to power up as well, if she felt the urge to instagram or tweet. "Wait a minute. If Sophie could call me, she has my number, won't they work out where I am from that?"

"Damn. You're right. Let's walk and talk." Walking outside wasn't the refreshing idea it should have been. The dry air scratched Marina's skin. They walked past bench seats and a picnic area, to a rocky bend in the river.

Cooper said, "You're gonna have to stop using it."

The phone? "But you only just gave it to me."

"Give it back," he held his hand out.

She refused.

"Marina, your parents are in such deep shit they exiled you to Australia to keep you out of trouble. This phone is trouble."

She still couldn't hand it over. Her one connection to the outside world and he wanted to take it off her?

Cooper pulled her into a hug. "Everything's going to be OK." Then, leaning back a little, he tucked his finger under her chin and lifted her face to his. Intimacy cloaked them. He pressed his lips to hers, the contact stealing all rational thought from her brain.

The kiss wound her nerves tight; sent her pulse sprinting. This memory would be seared into her brain for years. Everything fled her mind, only sensation mattered as she deepened the kiss, luxuriating in the intimacy of the moment. Her lips parted, letting him in, letting him closer.

Suddenly he pulled back and said, "Please give me the phone."

The shock hit her with a slap. "If I give this back, it will make you just as cruel as my parents."

Cooper held his hand out again. "We both know that's not true."

"But I won't last without a phone."

"I'll help you."

He held her and kissed her again. A little more pressure, a lot more wonderful. He filled her with hope, all the way through to her knees. If they kept going at this rate her feet would never touch the ground again. She'd never felt so protected and wanted. Could she trust Cooper?

When they eventually stopped kissing, she took the phone out of her pocket. It felt heavy in her hand. Her only connection to the outside world was the one thing that exposed her to the whole world as well. With an almighty surge of willpower, she pressed it into Cooper's hand.

She couldn't quite let go. As if the device was a part of her soul she couldn't part with.

"Say goodbye to the phone, Marina."

She looked up. "I don't want to."

He pulled it away from her. Standing up, he threw it, hard. It landed downstream with a plop.

Marina screamed.

Cooper held her tightly. "It's OK. I'll get you another one as soon as this is over."

"You threw it away! I would never have given it to you if I'd known you'd do that!"

"It's OK, calm down."

Red mist blurred Marina's vision. "I will not calm down!"

"No need to shout."

"I am not –" pulling up short, she took a calming breath. "Oh God damn it, I am shouting." She took a deep breath through her nose and then breathed out slowly from her mouth, doing her best to steady herself. "This is not your fault. You've been nothing but wonderful. My head keeps spinning."

"I've got you. Let's keep walking then. No thinking, let's just be tourists and enjoy the peace and quiet while it lasts."

He stopped as they reached the road, that turned

into a bridge across the river. Marina grabbed him and pulled him closer. She played with the collar of his shirt, her neck and face heating with anticipation of a serious make-out session. This close, his neck was lean but strong, the Adam's apple jutting and dipping as he swallowed. Tilting her head up, she lifted her gaze to his. Glazed, dilated pupils looked into hers. Awesome.

"You need to kiss away my troubles now," she said.

"I'll do my best."

The wonderful thing about kissing Cooper, he really did make her forget about everything else in the world. Only for a moment, but that's all she needed. Whether she moved in or he leaned forward didn't matter. Their lips met with a soft, intimate pressure that sent fuzzy sparkles through her bloodstream. Senses clamored for attention, from the inviting scent of him to the pressure of his arms holding her closer into his body. An involuntary noise escaped her throat as she adjusted her lips to his, loving the confident play of their mouths.

Eventually they both came up for air.

"What do I do now? I mean, what can I do? I still don't have any money, I'm stuck at the estate. I can't talk to my parents and the way I see this playing out, the media will find us any minute and then the police will most likely turn up."

"We should make a list. Work out the best way to clear your name, the pros and cons."

"I'm gonna need a lawyer."

Cooper coughed. "As it happens, My mom's a lawyer."

"Well, that's handy."

"Not really. She's a prosecutor. You need someone from the other side."

"Dang."

"The media are already here. I should do interview. To clear my name and set the record straight. You know the local scene, who should I give the exclusive to?"

"Will it mean telling the world what you know about your mom's paintings?"

"Yeah, it will. I have to clear my name. I can't just wait for the police to come and arrest me. I mean, that's what's eventually going to happen, isn't it? And even if they don't, at some point I'll need to leave Boomerang Estate and go home.'

His arm wrapped around her shoulders as he said, "Can I be honest?"

Uh-oh, that sounded ominous. She stopped walking and faced him. "You want to bail? I totally get why you'd want to bail. I want to bail, but I can't exactly bail on myself, can I?"

"Well," he took a slow breath, "You have kind of made me an accessory to art fraud."

"I didn't know it myself until the museum."

He looked at her with an unreadable expression.

Panic spiked through Marina. "You do believe me, don't you? Jesus, Cooper, if you don't believe me I may as well hand myself in right now.'

"I do believe you."

She let out a huge sigh. "I had no idea how much I needed to hear that just now. You're probably the only person in the world who believes me."

He slipped his arms around her waist and pulled her in closer, so her chest was touching his. "I was not going to bail. The opposite in fact.

***

True to her pattern, it was Pearl who found them. In a cafe, but not until they were up to dessert, so at least they'd had a meal and privacy first.

"Miss Beatrice is asking for you. So are several reporters. I said you were in our room with a headache."

"And they bought it?" Marina asked.

"Nobody is letting them in, and Taylah is hiding in the upstairs bathroom."

Cooper gave her an extra awesome kiss before they parted.

***

Copper drove them home to the estate. He stayed quiet, wondering whether the media would be there or not.

Marina, however, was as chatty as ever. "Pearl, tell me how this works. How come Miss B doesn't kick me out already?"

"I'm sure your tuition was already paid before she accepted you. Not that I'm privy to the finances."

Marina laughed. "I bet there's a first time for everything. Especially now my parents are all over the news."

"She'd never cast someone out."

Marina shook her head. "So why are you so nervous? You act like you could be expelled at any moment. She's got you on a tight leash that's for sure."

"I'll never get used to the way Americans voice their every thought," Pearl said as they approached the main gates.

The media scrum was still there. They turned as one in their direction. The wall of noise - questions, camera lights, bodies pressed together - became the most bizarre obstacle course. It was proving difficult to simply get the car doors open.

The plan was to hold their heads up, but they could barely see where they were going. Marina clung to Cooper's arm. Bodies jostled and pressed. The front door should only be a few meters ahead of them, but every step felt like it was taking them further away. They couldn't go back to the car now. Had to press on.

One of them shouted, "Marina! What do you say to all the people you ripped off?"

Another called out, "Are you sorry for what you've done?"

Moving as one, the reporters' questions buzzing filled their ears.

"Marina, were you involved in your parents' deception?"

"Why are you in Australia?"

"Little space here, I'm worried some of you will fall over!" Marina shouted.

Don't say anything.

"Please be careful," she said.

Be quiet!

"Watch your feet! That gear looks expensive!"

Hang on, it's working.

Saying nothing had made them press closer, but by offering help and assistance, for some reason they started to back off.

Somebody yelped as they slipped on the dusty ground.

"Are you all right?" Marina stopped and asked. She held her hand out to help the camera operator up.

Guilty people didn't stop to worry about hurt strangers. The footage would show Marina cared about people. This might play out in Marina's favor.

Cooper pulled the front door, Marina and Pearl stepped in. They closed the door and the noise behind them.

Safe!

A woman and a camera operator were sitting in the front room.

"You must be Marina. I'm Carmen Garcia from Network America."

His gut clenched, his mouth dried. He'd walked them straight into a trap.

Marina reached for his hand and squeezed. He squeezed it straight back. Carmen kept right on talking. "Miss Beatrice has granted me an exclusive."

CHAPTER 10

Every swear word in the universe tumbled inside Marina's brain, but none of them made it to her voice box, which had shut down. Body buzzing from shock, she couldn't feel her hands. Cooper reached across her and said something, but all was white noise.

"Marina, I'm offering you a great deal," Carmen said. "You want to tell the world what's really going on, I simply want an exclusive. We can help each other out here."

She wanted to be left alone. But she also wanted to tell everyone she had nothing to do with her parents' crimes. She needed the world to believe her.

Carmen pressed her advantage. "If you keep up this silence, the rest of the pack will be like a hungry dog gnawing on an old bone. They won't leave you alone."

Marina couldn't work out what made her angrier.

That the reporter was being so casual, or that she was right.

What if this never went away?

What if this was her life now?

"Think about what I'm offering. We can arrange payment once you sign on with us."

Sign on? It was all noise.

Carmen said, "We can do it all live, no editing, no frankenquotes. You get to tell the world what's really going on, in your own words. But the clock is ticking."

Marina reached for Cooper's hand and squeezed it again. Then she turned to him, "Will you be there with me?"

***

Cooper's phone bleeped. A message from Mom popped up.

Cooper dear, we're on a big case that is attracting media attention. If you are approached by anyone, say nothing.

Media advice? He had to laugh at the timing.

He replied: "Can't be as huge as the shitstorm breaking here?"

"Can't tell you. Sit tight. No Comment."

Then another message.

"And please don't swear."

She sent him nothing further about the 'big case' she was on. "Can you give me a moment?" He asked Marina as he moved to the corner of the room to do some media due-diligence. He searched his mother's name to see what news hits came up. He read the first one.

His heart plummeted to the floor. It had to be a mistake. The name Shenko was right there in the headline.

Belly filling with lead, he rubbed his forehead. Oh Jesus no.

This could not be happening.

This was too cruel!

He had to warn Marina, but as he turned around, she was talking to the reporter. Anything he said now would get blown sky-high.

If he hadn't thrown her phone away, he could have sent her a private message and been able to talk. Damn!

Honestly, he and Marina's lives would be so much less complicated if they'd been orphans!

Instead of being able to take her aside and explain what was going on, Marina was shaking hands with the reporter and Miss Beatrice was leading Marina towards the Library!

***

Just when Marina thought they'd get the interview at least started, if not over and done with, Miss Beatrice then requested a moment of Marina's time.

"This is my family home," she said, her face pale

with fear. "Please do not conduct the interview here. I do not want Boomerang Estate associated with scandal!"

"Take it easy. Nobody's going to care where the interview is happening, B."

"I care. Can you conduct it elsewhere, please? I do not wish my reputation to be associated with such tawdry news."

Tawdry? Marina would look that word up later.

Miss Beatrice chewed the inside of her cheek. "We live in a conservative world. People choose this school for the very reason it is secluded and discreet. Conducting the media through our doors associates the school with negative publicity."

Ready to tear her hair out, Marina paced the room. She stopped by the shelves – the ones she and Miss Pearl had re-arranged. Had it only been a few days ago? It felt like weeks. Did she dare expose the prim and proper lady's secrets?

How else to make the woman see reason?

"Miss Beatrice, I don't think this finishing school has such a squeaky-clean reputation to protect."

"What could you possibly mean?"

Growing bold, breathing heavily with a pounding heart, Marina took a hardcover book from the shelf and opened it to a random page. It had a late 19th century painting of a woman with her skirts high over her head and a man crouched between her legs. She showed the open page to the chatelaine. "You've got a library full of dirty books. Hardly suitable reading material for conserv-ative young women."

Miss Beatrice opened and closed her mouth like a fish.

Grabbing another book at random, Marina flicked the pages to find a cartoon of a man with his trousers around his knees while a newborn calf mistook his member for his mother.

"Who put these horrid books in here?" Miss Beatrice spluttered.

"That I don't know. But the library is full of them. All this time we've been balancing them on our heads to improve our posture."

Miss Beatrice grabbed at the wall to steady herself. "If anyone found out, my reputation would be in tatters."

"Like mine is now."

Miss Beatrice found a chair and sank into it. "Please. This is my livelihood. It's all I have. I know you've lost your career; but you're young, you can reinvent yourself."

"And this is exactly where I start to reinvent myself. I promise not to take the books down, but the room is perfect. It's cozy and warm, but not over the top. If we do the interview now, we get it done and then it's all over.

Miss Beatrice rubbed her forehead and breathed a few times. The always upright, perfectly postured woman visibly slumped. "You have to give me your word this will never get out."

"I can't promise you it will never leak out. But I can absolutely guarantee I certainly will never speak of it."

"Who else knows about these books?"

Something curdled in her stomach at betraying the confidence. "Pearl knows. It was an accident that we found them at all. After the walking with books on our head session, we were trying to match the dust jackets with the right books, except they didn't have titles on the front, so we opened them up to see. That's when we realized they were fake covers."

"I want your word that you will never tell a soul."

"You have it."

A knock sounded at the door. Miss Beatrice's eyes sprang open in shock. It had to be the reporter and her camera, wanting to get started.

"I'll get it, shall I?"

Not that Marina was particularly happy with the situation either, but she couldn't let Miss Beatrice know that. It was all about putting on a brave front, making this seem like this interview was her idea. If she wavered for a moment, Miss Beatrice would talk her out of it. And then they'd have the increasingly awful problem of reporters camped out in front of the chalet because Carmen had made it very clear she wasn't leaving without an interview.

Despite Marina's years of being in the public eye, a live interview was new territory, and it scared the living crap out of her.

She opened the door and welcomed Cooper in with

a hug that said she never wanted to let him go. Carmen then came in with her camera person and another woman they hadn't seen before – she wore a heavy corset-type thing around her waist and brought in boxes of lighting gear. It looked like they were setting up for a rock concert, not an interview.

Miss Beatrice looked at the vast boxes of gear and said, "You have one hour, you may use the library. Then you are to leave."

"Yes Ma'am," they chorused.

"My name is Miss Beatrice, not 'ma'am'," she said, then walked out.

Panic splashed over Cooper's face as he leaned into her ear. "We need to talk."

Carmen interrupted, "Patty, can we mike him up as well?"

***

Damn, they were 'hot miked' already. No good could come of this. If he said anything, it would be recorded. Not good. Very, very not good at all.

There had to be a way to talk to her, privately, to let her know about the tsunami of trouble heading their way. An impossible task.

"Are you sure you want to go through with this?" *Please change your mind. We can kick everyone out.*

"I don't really have much choice, do I? It's either talk to Carmen or be hounded by everyone else for however long this goes on for."

"We're ready now," Patty said.

Wow, that was quick!

Carmen said out loud for Cooper's benefit. "We'll be taping everything on the cameras, for later highlight packages, but we'll also be sending it out live on social."

"It's going live?" Cooper gulped.

"That way they can't stitch me up in editing." Marina said, giving his hand a squeeze.

The camera operator handed Cooper his mike pack. "Slip it on the back of your belt."

"I'm not in the interview," he protested.

"No, Cooper, I need you," Marina pleaded. "Do this with me. You don't have to say anything, just be next to me. I can't get through this without you."

Was there time to have a quick vomit first? Nope. No time to protest, only take a seat on the sofa next to Marina and pray this was over with real soon. What were the odds Carmen even knew who he was?

"Before we get started," Carmen said, handing them each a contract to sign.

The red light above the camera was already on. The camera phone was also trained on them. This was happening. For real.

"We get you two signing your agreements on camera, that way we're all protected," Carmen said. "You wouldn't believe the excuses people come up with after an interview goes out. 'I didn't know the cameras were on, I didn't know I was being interviewed, I thought we were just having a chat.' You name it, I've heard it."

Marina signed and handed hers back.

Having lawyer parents had trained Cooper to speed read the paper first, before he too signed and dated it.

Done.

Completely done.

Carmen handed the forms to Patty, who took photos of the documents with her phone.

Oh Jesus. He'd signed his name. When that document made it back to the network's head office, would they recognize his name? Maybe they'd file it and wouldn't even look. Sure, a lot of lawyers knew each other, but his parents were west coast and Network America was based in New York.

Pulse beating a tattoo inside his brain, he felt ice cracking under his feet. Any minute now he'd plunge through.

Marina smiled at him, gave his hand a squeeze and said, "Don't look so worried. Everything will be OK."

No, it really wouldn't be.

***

CHAPTER 11

Three cameras, in the end. An old-fashioned proper one that looked heavy (hence the support belts the operator wore). There was a phone camera as well, aimed at Marina, and the third camera was on a tablet device, its lens aimed at Carmen, but positioned so Marina could see the screen from where she sat. A mixture of angry and sad-face emojis drifted across the screen as they prepared to go live.

Starting from a negative position already? Tough crowd. Marina's stomach flipped. This was going to be a tough job turning people around.

"Marina Shenko," Carmen began, "Thank you for joining us here on Network America."

Hard to muster a smile when everything inside her turned rotten.

Marina's chin wobbled. "This is such foreign territory for me, Carmen." *I remembered her name!* "This is not the confident person people are used to seeing. But I'm so grateful for the chance to tell my side of the story." *Did I just talk about myself in the third person?*

Carmen nodded and said, "We're going out live across the world, everyone is welcome to post comments and questions. Before we get to our viewers questions, I have a few of my own. The one I guess everyone wants to know is this. How much did you know?"

Marina wanted to laugh, because the answer was so simple. "I didn't know anything. The first time I heard about it, I was already in here in Australia in the middle of bumf- I mean, the outback. Then I found out my parents were being raided. So really, I found out pretty much at the same time as everyone else."

Carmen's expression stayed neutral. It was clear she wanted Marina to say more, but Marina held back. *Don't fill the silence, don't fall for it, you'll end up saying way too much.*

"You didn't know your parents were frauds?"

A bit nasty so early on, but Marina remembered the woman was a reporter and she needed an angle. "I found out about the raids at the same time as everyone else. I had no idea it was coming."

"But the timing does look strange. Just before your parents are raided, you flee the country?"

"I didn't flee," Marina inwardly cursed at taking the bait. On the tablet screen, a new wave of angry emojis drifted across. She was being too cagey. Too short. She needed to take charge of this interview. "With hindsight, I'm only just now starting to put the pieces together. The thing is, I was brought to Australia and didn't have a clue what was going on. I unpacked my bags and didn't even have a phone, I had no way of contacting anyone. It's kind of funny now, but at the time, I had wondered if my parents were punishing me for my YouTube addiction or something. I was posting *a lot*."

A few yellow smiley face emojis competed with the red angry ones. Marina took that as encouragement to keep talking. "Here's the thing, I guess I'm a classic teenager, so wrapped up in myself and what I'm interested in, I didn't pay attention to what anyone else did. So, when I came to Australia, I thought it was all about me. Isn't that funny? I thought my parents were punishing me for being too caught up in my own world, that they thought I needed some digital detox or something. By the way, if anyone watching could cope without a phone or wifi for a week, give me the thumbs up, because I sure as heck couldn't! I was having withdrawal symptoms after barely an hour!"

Little blue thumbs sprinkled amongst the smiling faces, pushing away the angry ones. The screen was too far away for Marina to read people's comments or questions, but the colors were definitely changing in Marina's favor.

Carmen leaned forward and said, "You're sticking to the narrative that you didn't know. But I have to ask - and we're getting a lot of questions coming in on a similar theme - how could you *not* know? How come you didn't notice what your parents were up to?"

"It's a fair question, Carmen, but if I can just walk it back a little. I haven't spoken to my parents since before this blew up, and as far as I know, they haven't made any public statements. So, I think we should approach this, like everything else, from the presumption of innocence. I'm sure a lot of people have already decided my parents are guilty, but I think we should leave that decision to the courts. If it ever comes to that.

"But if you're asking how could I not know that they were about to be raided? If I were sitting at home watching this feed, I'd be wanting to know that too. In my defense, and this is by no means an excuse, I was incredibly self-absorbed. I had close to four million followers on the socials, my days were filled with entertaining them. So that's where I was coming from. Then I'm suddenly in in Australia - so given those circumstances . . . maybe my parents thought something bad was coming and they wanted to protect me and get me out of the way? I don't know, and I can't attribute motives to them because I haven't been able to speak to them at all."

"What would you say to your parents, right now? If they're watching this?"

"I'd say they should co-operate fully with authorities to sort this mess out."

Yellow smiley faces began to outnumber the angry red ones.

"Do you believe they're guilty?"

Now was not the time to throw them under the bus. "They're my parents and I love them."

"But do you think they're guilty?"

"Like I said, I've had no communications with them, and am just as in the dark about this everyone else."

"You're avoiding the question."

"They're my parents, I love them with all my heart. I'm also incredibly worried about them and my little brother. To answer your question, I think they're completely innocent."

"You know this for a fact?"

"I am so massively confused right now." Heat pressed in behind Marina's eyes. Any moment now the tears would come. "I'm missing a lot of information. There's a lot going on that I still need to unpack, but of course I am presuming their innocence. That's their right."

A mixture of smiley faces and angry faces drifted across the screen. She was winning some of them over, but not all of them. This would take a while.

Carmen continued her cross examination. "A number of your friends are claiming they were ripped off. Social media is in meltdown over the Shenko Fraud hashtag. What would you say to your friends who are watching? Your friends who have been ripped off?"

Marina had to clamp her lips together to stop the honesty gushing out. What she'd dearly love to say to her friends would be 'shut up' because none of their anger was helping the situation. "I'd say that I love them so much, and that I'm so sorry they're caught up in this mess, and that I hope it can all be sorted out really soon."

"Your friends have been ripped off."

Cooper squeezed her hand for support. For the shortest moment, she'd forgotten he was even there. Knowing he was right beside her gave her some extra courage.

"Being in Outback Australia right now has cut me off from everyone. If I was home now, I'd be giving my friends the biggest hugs and . . ." a heavy sigh came out, "to be honest, we'd probably all be crying and wondering what the heck was going on. Everyone is hurting right now, it's understandable that -"

"- You introduced them the world of art investments. Now their investments are worthless. Be honest. How do you live with yourself after that kind of a revelation?"

More angry faces than smiley ones drifted right to left.

She'd lost control of the interview from the first question. Now all she could do was hang on and hope it all ended soon. This wasn't helping anyone, least of all her.

"I understand the anger. I'd be angry too if I were them and it happened to me. Well, it has really. When you think about it, I've pretty much lost my parents because of this. I might lose a lot of my friends as well. But I'm not going to play the victim here. I'm looking forward to helping set everything back to rights."

This was getting so ugly, so messy.

"Setting things back to rights. That means things are not right, are they?"

Another deep sigh. "Obviously, I'm trying to be as careful as I can. I am certainly frustrated with everything that's going on." She couldn't say her parents had done the wrong thing because that would pre-suppose their guilt, even though she felt sure they probably had done something majorly shady.

"We're going round in circles a little," Carmen said. "And obviously nobody wants to prejudice a potential court case, or be the reason a trial is aborted. So, let's get onto safer ground. What is your involvement in all this?"

"You know what? My involvement is zero. None at all. Like I said before, I was pretty self-absorbed. I probably still am." She tried to make a joke at her own expense. She'd read somewhere that people who did that tended to be seen as likable. "Can you imagine being me for a moment? Just imagine people accusing your parents of ripping people off, of saying you had to be part of it. I still don't even know the full extent of what they've been accused of. I don't know if they've even been charged yet. I am *completely* in the dark here, literally on the other side of the world. I used to have my own life, I used to be successful in my own right, I had a great social media thing going, and then overnight it's gone."

"Your parents are about to be charged," Carmen said. "It will most likely be fraud and deception charges. You yourself may be charged as an accessory."

Like pulling a plug, all her strength drained out. A quiet little, "aw shit," escaped.

"There's something else coming up a lot in the public questions," Carmen said.

"OK," Marina barely heard her, too busy processing.

"This lovely gentleman beside you. Cooper Den Brave."

"He's been my rock." Her hand gave his a squeeze. "So wonderful through this."

A scattering of love hearts drifted across the screen.

Maybe the tide was turning?

"How did you two meet?"

Marina turned and looked his way, he made a shy smile back. For a second she was about to blurt out their story, but an invisible string pulled at the back of her head and she stopped herself. "Do you know what? This is going to sound weird. I've pretty much lived my whole life in the public eye. Everything is social media or it doesn't happen. But . . . what's going on with us . . . this is so new and fresh and kind of confusing but also really nice, that for the first time in my life I think I'd like to keep something private."

The screen filled with love hearts.

"That's adorable," Carmen said. Then she held her phone and checked another question. "This is fascinating. Cooper, people are saying your mother is one of the investigators prosecuting the case in LA. Is that true? And if so, how much conflict does this place you in? I assume your parents know who you're dating?"

White noise filled Marina's head. The screen, previously filled with love hearts, became clogged with the laughing-so-hard-I'm-crying emoji. Her heart smacked against her ribs, her stomach roiled. All she could do was look at Cooper and wonder what the hell had just happened.

Oh Jesus oh Jesus oh Jesus oh Jesus this can't be true.

A squeaky, "Did you know this?" slipped out. Marina knew her face must be giving everything away, but she didn't have the strength to steady her features.

In a soft voice, Cooper said, "As soon as I found out, I wanted to tell you, but . . ." He waved his hand in the general direction of all the interview equipment.

"There you go," Marina blurted as she turned back to Carmen. "Surely this proves that I didn't know what any of the people in my life were doing. Or are doing." She was almost proud of herself for that recovery. Except she wanted to puke.

If there was a dumpster fire emoji, it would be floating across the screen right now.

The rest of the humiliating interview eventually came to a stop. Cooper was saying something but she didn't hear it. The desperate need to be alone eclipsed everything else.

He pulled her aside and kept talking. Eventually a few words penetrated the fog of her brain.

"I promise you, I didn't know they were working on the case."

"But . . . how did you *not* know?"

He pulled her directly into his line of sight. "You're asking me how I didn't know what my Mom was working on? That's rich coming from you."

The last vestiges of her ego splintered onto the floor.

"I shouldn't have said that," Cooper pulled her into an embrace. "I'm sorry that was unfair."

Marina pushed him away. He said something but she only heard noise. Somehow, she made to the little room she shared with Pearl. Then she fell on her bed and curled into a tight ball of grief and confusion.

Cramming her eyes shut, she waited for the inevitable tears. Something malfunctioned in her brain, because the tears stayed in. Body shaking and numb, she grabbed the top blanket and crammed the fabric into her mouth. Now she could howl without alerting the rest of the chalet.

Somebody was patting her on the shoulder, muttering vague Pearl-type noises which didn't translate into complete words. Marina rocked into her body, making herself smaller. The room darkened, somebody closed the door and came back to sit on the bed. A hand rubbed her back in soothing swirls.

"You poor thing." She said.

That Pearl. What a keeper.

Marina needed her Mom. But if Mom really was here, she'd scream at her for trashing her life.

She hated Mom right now.

Yet she missed her so much.

"You stay here all tucked up. I'll make you a cup of tea." Pearl said.

It was hard to focus. "Everything is fuzzy."

"You're probably in shock. I'll make the tea extra sweet."

The footsteps moved away and the door closed.

Loneliness consumed Marina. Warm salty tears leaked out, seeping into her mouth on the way down, soaking into the pillow and bedding. The whoosh and whirl of her pulse filled her ears, sucking her body into a washing machine of insecurity.

She shouldn't have talked to the media.

But not because of her parents. Cooper was the reason she shouldn't have talked to them. Everything was going fine until someone had made the connections between her parents and his.

Great going there, pouring gas onto a flame!

He'd said he didn't know, but he must have. But then she hadn't known what her parents had been up to either. Everything was seriously messed up.

The door opened.

"Here's your tea. I wasn't sure if you took milk so I've brought a little jug."

The phrase, 'thank you,' was on her tongue, but all that came out was an anguished howl.

"Sit up, it's too hard to drink sideways and I don't have any bendy straws."

Pearl put it all on the little side table, then slipped an arm under Marina's shoulder and helped her lean up against the pillows. A moment later she grabbed the pillows off her own bed to add them to Marina's supportive pile. Then she moved to walk out.

A pathetic little, "Don't leave me," crept out.

"I thought you'd want some privacy?"

She adored the way Pearl said it. PRIVV-a-see, instead of her usual PRY-vase-ee "Don't like being left with my thoughts."

"Shall I open the blinds?"

Such a basic question, but Marina's synapses refused to fire, leaving her unsure of the most basic things. "I don't know . . . maybe?"

She sipped the tea. Hot and sickly sweet, like flat soda. Only hot.

"I'm sorry the interview went so badly," Pearl said. "I completely believe you, by the way. So do the rest of the girls. We're all on your side. OK?"

That set off a fresh burst of tears. Pearl was beside Marina in a heartbeat, moved the tea out the way and embraced her. "Just keep remembering, 'this too shall pass'. It won't feel like it right now, but it will get better."

A chocked sob. "When?"

"That we don't know. But it will. One day. Right now, you're bruised and hurting, but little by little, it will get better."

"I shouldn't have done the interview."

"There, there."

A shuddering sigh came out. "The papps wouldn't leave me alone."

"I've been there, trust me."

Marina sniffed. "You have?"

The rubbing stopped. Pearl sighed heavily. "I may as well tell you now. I'm properly famous in Britain, don'tcha know?"

"You are?"

"Yeah. Can't move for the papps. That's why I came here, to get a break. I nearly died when I saw the cameras out the front. Thought they'd finally found me. Can't tell you how relieved I was when I heard they were here for you instead."

Nothing made sense, what with her synapses shutting down and her body developing a fresh set of shakes. But the back rubs were nice and comforting and the tone of Pearl's words were so soothing. And at least nobody was asking her any more questions and the cameras were gone.

The microphone!

Rubbing her chest, she expected to feel the wire. Relief washed over her, it was all gone.

"What's wrong?" Pearl asked.

"I thought I was still wearing the mike."

"Wouldn't put it past them, sneaky buggers."

It brought a glint of relief into Marina's gloomy world. She reached for a tissue and wiped her face, blew her nose, then picked up the tea again. "So, you reckon this works?"

"Oh yes. Good cup of tea fixes everything."

Marina shrugged. "If you say so." Taking another sip, she winced at the sweetness. There was something bitter in the aftertaste. Perhaps she should put milk in it after all.

Or she could pull herself together and make a coffee.

Not that her body was in any shape to comply. Everything ached. Her muscles, and bones, even her hair pushed against the grain.

"I think you should get some sleep." Pearl said.

"But it's too early."

"It's OK. Miss Beatrice will understand. Get a good rest and you'll feel better in the morning."

Marina curled down into the bed, then remembered. "Oh wait, Pearl. I have to tell you. Miss B knows about the books."

"What? How did she find out about the mucky pictures?"

Guilt-weight sagged her body. "I told her."

"Why ever did you do that?"

It had seemed like such a good idea at the time, but now it was one more poor decision she'd made. "She didn't want me to do the interview in the library, so I told her about the books and that I . . . It doesn't matter. She knows. And she knows you know as well."

"Right." Pearl said.

That was all she said.

"Go on, scream at me, you may as well."

"Not much point." Pearl shrugged. "You're already

beating yourself up about everything else. I won't add to it."

"That means so much," Marina said with a sniff.

Pearl giggled. "Not sure I'll ever be able to look at her the same way again, though."

The world had not stopped spinning, much to Marina's displeasure. The proof came as Pearl's bed squeaked with her getting up. How did she managed to get up so consistently early without an alarm going off? Did she have some kind of ESP body clock or something?

"Oh my gosh you have a phone?" Marina sat bolt upright.

Pearl tucked the device unto her bra. "Hush now, I'm off to prep breakfast. I'll put some *kummerspeck* on for you."

"I'm coming with you." Marina threw the covers off. She was still mostly dressed from crawling into bed yesterday afternoon. Whatever time it was, she'd slept enough. "By the way, what's *kimmel shpet?*"

Pearl gave her a huge smile. "Kummerspeck is a German word I picked up a few years back, it translates as 'grief bacon', and we all know bacon makes everything better." Then she pulled herself up short. "Oh my gosh, I never thought to check if you're vegetarian?"

"Nope, so bacon me up."

In the kitchen, they got to work preparing breakfast for the residents.

The chunks of bacon sizzled in the pan. "It's a lot thicker than I get back home," Marina said.

"It's a different cut, it's so deliciously fatty."

Marina's belly folded in on itself. "Are you sure it's safe to eat?"

"Oh yes. Just make sure you drink lashings of orange juice with it, to cut down the fat."

Marina sliced apples into thick chunks, as Pearl directed, then added them to the pan. It might not look all that great, but is sure smelled delicious.

The smell wafted from the kitchen into the dining room as Marina set the tables. Prithee and three other residents wandered in early, sniffing the air.

"Can we help?" Prithee asked.

"All good. I'll get the kettle on so you can have coffee."

"And tea," Prithee added. "And Marina, I'm so sorry about yesterday."

"Oh." Marina's belly sank. "You saw it?"

"We all did," Prithee said.

"Just you or . . .?"

"All the residents watched from Miss Beatrice's private lounge."

"Oh."

"That was a stitch-up if ever I saw it," Prithee said.

"But we believe you," one of the others said.

Marina hadn't gotten around to learning her name.

Which, now she thought about it, was incredibly rude and self-involved. In other words, typically Marina.

She'd fix that, starting right now. "I can't tell you how glad I am to hear that. Or that you haven't secretly voted to cast me out or something."

A worried look crossed everyone's faces.

Oh.

"I've decided that from now on I'm going to be useful. How do you all take your coffee?"

"Make mine tea, white with one sugar," Prithee said.

Marina nodded.

The next girl said, "same," and Marina nodded.

This was going great!

CHAPTER 12

A message buzzed on Cooper's phone. Bleary eyed, he read the first line and woke up rapidly.

Please attend the sessions you're booked in for. We have many patients on our waiting list who would gladly take your spot.

Text messages had a way of sounding blunt and pissy even when it wasn't intended, but he was pretty sure whoever typed this was pissed.

Guilt - not much, but it was there - flickered to life. He shouldn't care, he really shouldn't. His parents were paying for the sessions, not him. They were the ones who booked them in the first place.

Eases their guilt for never being around.

Whoa, where had that thought come from?

The thought burrowed in like a tick and grew.

He checked the time. He had half an hour to get to his next appointment. Suddenly he wanted to go.

———

"Good, you got my message," the receptionist said as he arrived in the office.

"Loud and clear," Cooper said, heading to the sofa. Such a cliche having a sofa to lie down on. As if someone would lie back and talk about their childhood, and all the problems of the world would magically disappear.

"Don't take the lounge," she said. "Sit in my seat, you're going to be me."

"We're doing role play now?"

"Sit. I'm going to be you." She sat on the lounge, man-spread her legs comically wide and played on her phone.

He sat in her chair and shook his head. "This is stupid."

"Aww dis is stuupid," she said.

"I don't sound like that."

"Pahhk the cahhh in the garahhhhge."

"Stop it, why are you going all bogan on me?"

"I'm just warming up." She pretended to chew gum, really warming to the role. "I'm a poor little rich kid. My parents ignore me. They waste my time, so I waste their money. How do ya like dem apples?"

Anger took over Cooper. "This is a dick move."

"What is? Me pretending to be you, or you wasting everyone's time by not showing up to your sessions?"

He slumped. "OK, ya got me. Now can we actually have a session?"

"Gladly." She scrolled through her phone and checked something. "It's been a while since you've been here, and in the three sessions you did come to, you really didn't tell me much. So, I think I should continue to be you and you be me, and tell me the advice you really need to hear."

"Is this what you do when you run out of ideas? Get the patients to heal themselves?"

She smiled broadly and leaned back. "Patients generally own their journeys when they make their own plans, leading to making their own progress. I could tell you what to do, but until you decide, in your own words, what to do - it won't work."

"So, what is it exactly that you do then?"

"I get you to talk about what's bothering you. The first couple of sessions are a little like a chicken scratching at a pile. They don't uncover much, they're just starting to dig. It's really only a few sessions in that you dig down enough to find the real reason for your unhappiness."

"Obviously we're going to end up blaming my parents, aren't we?"

She smiled and said, "It's what you're doing now, isn't it?"

Leaning back in the chair, Cooper stared at the ceiling. He kept right on staring, then asked, "Can I still be you for a moment?"

"If it helps."

A grin formed, but he kept looking up, so he didn't have to look at her pretending to be him. Because a woman with legs spread like that sent all the wrong signals. "Ya gotta stop waiting for your folks to have time for you. They never did in the past, so they're not likely to start now."

"Keep digging."

"Skipping your shrink is a dick move. There are so many other ways of getting back at your parents who never have any time for you."

"Nice."

Cooper smiled, warming to his topic. "Being a raging success would be the best way to deal with the situation. Then I'd be too busy for *them*."

Now that he'd said it out loud, it sounded like a solid plan. He looked down again, expecting the counselor to laugh at how simplistic he sounded.

She wasn't laughing. She nodded and looked happy. "That sounds like a breakthrough."

A weight lifted off of him. But he wasn't going to admit it. He was just warming to the topic.

She said, "You slipped pretty quickly into the new role I threw at you, just then."

"Didn't have much choice."

She waited for more.

Damn, she was good. "It's the position I found myself in, so I adapted to it."

She nodded.

He shrugged. "You're going somewhere with this?"

She raised her brows, silently asking a question.

Time stretched.

"Ahhhh, I get it, I'm a pretender. Pretending to be something I'm not."

She wrote down some notes on her scribble pad and smiled at him. "That's almost it."

"Everybody pretends, don't they? It's all 'fake it till you make it' and all that."

"I'm familiar with the phrase. I was hoping you'd elaborate on how that applies to you?"

Cold guilt shut him down. "What ... what am I supposed to say?"

"Anything we talk about in here is strictly confidential. You're encouraged to be as candid as possible. The more honest you can be with yourself, the more value you'll obtain from these sessions."

Cooper's posture slumped and he shook his head. "It was never deliberate. It wasn't like I took anyone's job or anything. And I'm not outright claiming anything ..."

"It just sort-of-happened?"

"Well, kind of. I mean, I never said to anyone that I was indigenous, they just kind of assumed, and I ... didn't correct them."

"And now you have a job where even more people

might assume that connection to country and ... are you setting them straight?"

Honesty time. The woman was brutal. "I haven't been." No wonder he'd been avoiding her, when she peeled him open like this. "It's not good, is it?"

"It doesn't appear to have done any lasting damage to anyone, but if it went on for much longer, it might."

"I guess you're right."

"Would you like to lead a more honest life, then?"

"Well, yeah, I mean, doesn't everyone?" If only he knew something about her, he could hit back with whatever he knew. But she was incredibly good at masking. He hadn't even been able to find out anything on social media – and he'd searched! "You'd make an excellent spy," he said. "No, not a spy. An interrogator. Who do you really work for?"

She gifted him a smile and said, "I'm here to help you find the answers that are already within you. That's why I ask questions, and that's why you answer them. So let's get back to me asking the questions. How about this. You told me your parents investigate fraud. Is it possible that your actions – whether deliberate or not – are some way of gaining their attention?"

"Yeah, but it's art fraud."

"I know. I saw the interview."

He cringed. "That wasn't an interview, it was an ambush."

There was so much more he wanted to explore. "I think I'd better turn up to the next session."

She tilted her head. "Are you sure you need one?"

"I can't be cured already?"

She made a little 'squinch' with her face and said, "We tend not to use terms like 'cured', our sessions are more an exploration of ideas."

"But 'dick move' is ok?"

Now she smiled. "That's the very latest psychological terminology."

***

Marina cleared away the breakfast bowls and stacked them in the dishwasher. Thanks to Pearl's help through the morning, she'd memorized everyone's name. If she didn't know better, she'd say she was making some kind of personal connection.

Miss Beatrice inspected the kitchen. "Miss Marina, Miss Pearl, well done both of you on an excellent service this morning. We're started the day on the right foot at last. Miss Marina, if I didn't know better, I'd say hospitality was your calling."

The old Marina would have hated being compared to 'the help' and said something rude. The new Marina took a breath, smiled and silently counted to three. There was nothing wrong with receiving a compliment for hosting a satisfying meal.

"Thank you, Miss Beatrice," Marina said.

Miss Beatrice gave a sharp nod and turned around to walk out.

Huh? Not that Marina was expecting a total love in - it was just breakfast after all - but could the woman give them a smile at least?

"Maybe something got lost in translation," Pearl murmured.

"I'm trying to like her, but she keeps putting the walls up."

"So I've noticed."

Marina sighed and looked about the messy kitchen. So much work still to do. "I'll chuck the food scraps in the trash if you wipe the benches."

Pearl shook her head. "Oh dear me no. There's far too much food left over to throw out." Then she tutted something about Americans being wasteful.

"Hey, I'm still new at this 'being useful' stuff. You shall have to take me under your wing, dear Yoda, and teach me everything you know."

"Who's Yoga?"

Marina blinked. "Yoda. You know, from Star Wars. You're supposed to call me 'Young Padawan' and say something like, 'learn patience, you must' and all that."

Pearl shook her head and set about gathering storage containers for the leftovers. "I've never seen Star Wars."

"You what?"

"When you work eighteen hour days on a soap, there isn't time for any other TV shows."

"They're movies."

"Them too."

"But you've seen Harry Potter, right? What am I saying, you're a Brit, you were probably in it."

She grimaced. "Cutting room floor."

"Oh darling!" Marina embraced Pearl, "That's so cruel."

"It is rather a sore point. I tried for a role, but my contract with *Destination Street* still had two years to go and they wouldn't let me break it. So I took a smaller part that we worked on at night. I had a driver pick me up from Dessy - that's what we all call *Destination Street* - and I'd sleep in the car on the way to the night shoot. Then I'd do my muggle work and then another driver would take me back to Dessy and I'd get another hour's kip there."

"That sounds brutal."

"They noticed how tired I was so the writers had my character taking drugs to explain it. They love writing a 'good girl turned bad'.

"I gotta check out *Destination Street*."

"Please don't. Those days are long behind me."

"But you're so young! And you're beautiful - even if you could do with a little sun."

"Nope. Not going back. Had enough of being chewed up and spat out."

Marina gave her another hug. "Aren't we a pair. I wanted my fame back so much and you don't want anything to do with it."

"Riiiight," Pearl set about packing the leftovers. "Wait a minute, you just spoke in past tense. Does that mean you don't want your fame back?"

"Wow, did I say that?"

"You totally did."

"Must have been a fraudulent slip."

Laughter bubbled from Pearl. "I think you mean Freudian slip."

"Do I? OK then."

Now that she thought about it, Marina was starting to think a new life without the fame could be something worth aiming for. If only she knew what she could be good at.

CHAPTER 13

In the week since he'd last seen Marina, Cooper settled into a ... not exactly good, but at least some kind of routine. He had morning shifts at Boomerang, where he looked after the horses and sometimes ran a class ... but Marina never showed up to them. Then he'd have a session with the counselor, and spend the rest of the afternoon working out. Working out helped pass the time, but the pain also felt like he deserved it. Exercise released endorphins, apparently, but they were taking their sweet time turning up.

The counselor was helping. Instead of ditching his sessions, he slotted in more. His parents were paying for it so he may as well put their money to good use.

Marina was always in his thoughts.

And the media were still hanging around the front gates to Boomerang. Who knew how long their lenses were? They might be hundreds of meters away, but the lenses zoomed in so close they'd catch him changing his mind.

Today, he sweated out his frustrations and was looking forward to a decent shower. When he got back to his apartment, that same car was out the front as usual. It had to be a photographer in there. Instead of looking towards the car, he got his keys ready so that he could get in the front door as soon as possible.

Knock him sideways, not one but two parents were already in there when he walked in the door. Even more surprising, they were both looking his way, as if they'd been *waiting* for him to come home. Wait, it was his place, wasn't it? Had he become so burnt-out he'd driven all the way home to Sydney? Nah, the fires were still blocking the roads.

"Is everything all right?" He said as he walked in. "You look worried."

"Cooper darling, it's good to see you." His mother came towards him, one arm holding a glass of red wine, another outstretched for an embrace.

"I really am in trouble." He kissed his mother hello and hugged his father. Because that's what good sons did. "Has something bad happened?"

Dad smiled and shook his head. "I know, right? All three of us here at once. The world must be tipping on its axis."

"I take it you saw the interview?"

His parents looked at each other and then back at him, both of them grimacing.

Cooper said, "That'll be a 'yes' then." Were they going to offer him a drink as well or make him endure this reunion sober?

"Well, as you, ah, discovered, during that interview," his mother began. "I'm prosecuting the Shenko case, and you seeing Marina places me in a position of conflict. Can you confirm you're not seeing her anymore?"

The words *Not by choice* sprang to mind. Not that he'd tell them that. "She really doesn't know anything about what her parents did. And as I hardly ever see you guys, I can't see what the conflict is."

"That may be so," his father said. "But there is still the appearance of a conflict, and that could get the case thrown out before it even begins. Think about how much damage that could do to your mother's career."

Mom interrupted. "Darling, we really shouldn't talk about the case at all."

"Seriously? We're doing this again?" Cooper asked.

"You know we have to be incredibly careful with anything we say about this," Mom said. "If we don't tell you, that means you can't accidentally tell someone else. We've probably said too much as it is already."

Cooper shook his head and reached for a beer in the fridge. When had his parents ever had a set of keys to his place? "You are never going to let me forget that are you?"

"Son," Dad said in his most Dad voice, "You have caused a mistrial for your mother before."

"I was seven years old!"

Mom put her hands on her hips. "You told your class about my case for 'show and tell' and the defendant's nephew was in your grade!"

"And I *didn't know*! Jesus!" He took a swig, it tasted nasty. Not even alcohol was his friend today.

"Obviously, the less you say, the better it will be for everyone," Dad said.

Cooper knew how this played out. It always ended the same way. Maybe this time he'd cut to the chase and save himself the energy of enduring another lecture. They were trying to act concerned about natural justice and all that, but deep down what they were really worried about was that he might put dent in their ambitions.

He put his drink down on the bench. His father immediately picked it up and slid a coaster underneath. As if it were still their place.

"Well ain't that a thing." He headed for the bathroom and a hot shower. Because he still had a funky smell from the workout.

"You're being incredibly selfish again," his father called out behind him as Cooper reached the bathroom door.

"I'm not. I'm doing you both a favor by not talking to you. Then there can't possibly be any conflict, perceived or otherwise."

After the shower, all Cooper could think about was finding Marina.

Going via the front door was out of the question. Too

many media people still camped outside - despite that reporter, Carmen's earlier assurances that once they'd done an interview it would all go away.

The back window it had to be. He mis-timed the drop to the ground and jarred every joint in his body. Breathing through his teeth, he grabbed the horizontal pole of the clothes line and stretched his back out. Something clicked, so that had to be good.

His phone buzzed, his father was sending a detailed text message. Probably full of all the admonishment they hadn't achieved face to face.

Son, before you walked away, we had wanted to discuss the internship at the museum. It's a prestigious appointment and we know it will do you the world of good.

He felt that barb.

Your mother and I need to head back home, but we want your assurance you'll behave yourself and see the internship through to the end.

. . .

Excellent, his parents weren't expecting him to go home with them. That was a relief of sorts. He texted back:

If you two weren't such power freaks and only concerned about yourselves, you would have asked me how it's going and I would have told you in all honesty that I love it here. I like the museum, but you don't have to do me any favors...

Cooper blew out a steamy breath, deleted the entire message and instead texted:

I'd love a gig at the museum.

The reply:

Great to hear, I'll send them a letter of support.

He switched his phone off so he couldn't be tempted to type something else. Even when they were happy for him, his parents managed to tack on a veneer of disappointment.

Frustration bubbled through his veins. He'd really liked the museum he'd taken the Boomerang Estate residents to. It had been a great day, until Marina's freak-out.

Of course, his brain snagged on Marina again. And how much he desperately wanted to see her.

Again.

———

Marina's heart leapt into her mouth every time a book slid off one of the ladies' heads. Would it fall open on an explicit page?

Thump - oh thank goodness it fell and closed shut.

Thump - again, the pages closed shut.

Hooray for hard cover books, who knew they were self-closing?

She and Pearl had to avoid looking at each other in case they burst into giggles. And she couldn't look anywhere near Miss Beatrice's face because she knew what was in those books. But did anyone else?

After the posture session, Marina and Pearl remained behind and slotted the books into their fake dust jackets and placed them back on the shelves.

The spines on this row of books were all the same height, reminding Marina of prison bars.

"I think," Marina started as she placed the last book on the shelf. "I think I'd better hand myself in."

Pearl asked, "To whom?"

"The police, of course."

"But you haven't done anything wrong."

"Well, no, I haven't. But I can't stay inside the chalet all day and night. I'm going a little stir crazy. The media know I'm here - they're still camped outside and I'm stuck in here. I think I'd much rather go to the police and hand myself in than have the police come here and arrest me in front of the cameras."

"But . . . you said in the interview you didn't know anything." Pearl said. "And I believed you. We all did."

Marina let out a huge sigh that had been waiting to come out. "I know, and I didn't. I told the truth in the interview. I didn't know what they were doing. But maybe I was in denial. Maybe I did have a clue, and I chose to look the other way."

"Is that what really happened?"

"I don't know. But I want to be in control of my life again, rather than hiding here. Only guilty people hide, don't they? I'm going to hand myself in to the police and let them know I'm available to be interviewed and offer to help in any way I can."

"Gosh, you're brave."

"I don't feel brave. Will you come with me? Hold my hand, that sort of thing? Remind me I'm doing the right thing when I lose my nerve."

Pearl gulped.

Marina wavered. "Please come with me?"

"Do I have to?" Pearl chewed away at her bottom lip. "What about we invite the police to come here instead?"

Marina tilted her head to the side. "Why are you scared of the cops? What have you done?"

Now it was Pearl's time to sigh. "Nothing, obviously, it's just that I was really enjoying being out of the spotlight. It was so invigorating being 'normal' for a while."

"Ha!" Marina grabbed Pearl in a hug. "Normal's so overrated."

———

Saying you're going to hand yourself into police was one thing. Actually doing it required far more courage than Marina had. Pearl made her some coffee and brought it up to their shared bedroom. After Marina's first sip, her body gave in to shakes.

Pearl said, "I may have some chocolate somewhere. There's cocoa down in the pantry."

"No, I can't eat."

"You're so stressed, maybe we should do this tomorrow instead?"

That would only delay the inevitable. "I have to get this over with now, otherwise I'll never do it."

They heard the familiar splat-thunk of dusty earth hitting the window.

Could it be Cooper?

Marina wanted to run to him and hold him forever.

She also wanted to run a thousand miles away from him and never see him again.

What a mess!

Pearl said, "Shall I open the window to invite him in or politely tell him to fuck off?"

Marina burst into giggles at the swear word dropped in amongst Pearl's ever-so-posh accent. "But how do we let him in without the media going berserk?"

Pearl gave a confident smile. "We do have a back door, you know, right past the kitchen to the mudroom where we keep the bins."

Marina shook her head blankly.

"Oh, that's right, you call them trash cans."

The two of them walked to the back door and Pearl stuck her head out, made a whistle and ducked back inside.

The moment Cooper walked in, Marina's mouth turned dry. Everything she wanted to say deserted her.

Cooper spoke first. "I came here to make a groveling apology," he said. "I wanted to make a grand romantic gesture in front of the papps, but given the circumstances I think you'd prefer something private?"

Only some of what he said went in. She was still so angry and confused about what went down during her humiliatingly live interview. But thank heavens he hadn't done anything stupidly public. That would be ... well, stupid.

"I don't hate you," came out of her mouth. Only now did she realize it was the truth. She didn't hate him. "But we also can't pretend that what happened in the inter-view didn't happen."

"Phew!" He grabbed a seat and plonked himself down. "For a while there I wasn't sure if you ever wanted to see me again."

"For a while there I wasn't sure either."

Cooper made a grimace. "Fair enough, I deserved that."

"Uh, Marina?" Pearl was still in the kitchen.

They both turned to look at her.

"If we're going to head off, we probably need to do it now, otherwise we'll miss our window and I do have a rather lot of chores to be getting on with."

Confusion creased Cooper's face. "Where are you going? Not back to New York?"

That thought hadn't entered Marina's brain. All things considered, she really didn't have much of a plan at all really. "No I'm . . ." The truth of her situation hit her. "I can't anyway, I still don't have a passport. Or any money. What if - what if the police ask for ID to prove I'm who I say I am? What if they don't believe me."

"The Police?" Cooper asked.

Pearl cut in. "Marina wants to be on the front foot and hand herself in to the police before they come knocking the door down in front of the media."

"Let me help." Cooper said.

"That's right, your Mom's a lawyer," Marina bit back.

"Ouch." Cooper rubbed his chest where her verbal arrow struck. "I guess I deserved that."

Marina buried her face in her hands. "I have to do something but I'm too scared to move."

"Come on love, you can't sit down here all day." Pearl touched her on the shoulder. "It's either off to The Bill with you, or you help me with the laundry."

There was a third option. "Can't I go back to bed?"

"Suit yourself," Pearl huffed and walked out.

Tears built as Marina watched her leave.

"Now there's some tough love," Cooper said. "If this is what she's like when she's on your side, I'd hate to be her enemy."

The tears fell out. Marina buried her face in her hands. "I'm so scared, I really don't know what to do."

Cooper stepped closer, resting his hand on her shoulder. She fell into his body for a hug. He made some shushing noises and rubbed her back. "It's OK to be scared. And I think, deep down, you do know what to do."

Marina sniffed and wiped her face. "That's why I'm so scared."

CHAPTER 14

"My name is Marina Shenko, and I'm voluntarily handing myself in so that you know where I am, and that I'm not in hiding."

"What crime are you admitting to?"

"I haven't committed a crime. I'm just letting you know I'm not hiding, if anyone wants to speak to me."

The constable tilted her head and chewed her lip. "And you are?"

"I'm Marina Shenko. My parents are the art frauds."

"I'll get the sarge."

Marina and Cooper exchanged glances and she couldn't help wonder if this too was some kind of elaborate prank.

The Sarge, a woman in her forties, hadn't heard of Marina either. They sat in her office while the officer waited on hold, to get put through to the fraud squad.

"So, what crime are you admitting to?" Sarge asked.

"I didn't do anything."

"OK, because you're handing yourself in, and usually people don't hand themselves in to police for a crime they haven't committed."

Marina racked her brain. "That's the problem. I don't know if I've committed one or not."

Exasperated, the police woman shook her head. "We could charge you with wasting police time if you'd like."

Cooper interrupted. "Marina is from the Shenko family of New York. Her parents have been arrested for art fraud. We believe police from New York may be looking for Marina to question her in relation to her parents' alleged crimes –"

The officer held her hand up as the phone call finally connected to the right department in Sydney. After a while she turned back to Marina and got her address and phone number. She also asked for her passport, at which point Marina had to admit she didn't have one.

"How did you get here if you don't have a passport?"

"My mother came with me, then she put me in a taxi and went straight home. She must have taken it with her. I was too jetlagged to notice."

T wo hours later, having cleared up all their issues including the horrifying prospect that Marina would have to hand herself in to the immigration department. They could hardly go to Sydney anyway, there were still fires burning.

"Right," the woman sighed, "At least you're not a flight risk. What's your current address?"

"I'm staying at Boomerang Estate over on–"

"–Give them my address," Cooper said.

Wait, what? "You'll be the go-between?"

"No, I mean . . ." Cooper held Marina's hand and rubbed his thumb across her knuckles. "Stay with me instead."

"You're asking me to move in with you? Or have I read that all wrong and you're just trying to fix everything again?"

The sergeant cleared her throat. "We're not making reality tv here."

Cooper ignored her and said to Marina, "I wouldn't dare try and fix anything. But I'll help you any way I can."

Heat burned the back of Marina's eyes. "Thank you." *Oh God, don't cry!*

With a screech of metal on parquet floor, Cooper pushed his chair back and knelt at Marina's feet, still holding her hand. "I can't help," his voice cracked and dropped lower, "wanting to help . . . the people I love."

The third person in the room said, "Give me a break."

Marina's breath caught and happy tears poured out.

"You love me?" Nobody had ever said that before. Not for real, anyway. They'd said it when they were all together at a party, or fans would declare it to her in the street - but they were strangers. Their declarations of love didn't count. But this one did, because for the first time in her life, the words rang true. And she knew they were true because she felt like saying it back.

"Take it outside," the sergeant said.

"This is important," Marina said, not taking her eyes off Cooper as she wiped tears off her cheek.

"So are police resources." The woman said. "Give me the address and a contact phone number and you can be on your way."

The woman's comment broke through Marina's love-haze. "Oh my gosh, I nearly forgot, I want to help the police."

The woman raised her brows. "Yes, so you've said."

"No, I mean, *really* help. I don't mean to boast, but I'm all over social media. And I know a fair bit about art. And Cooper here, he's a total expert, he knows heaps. Give our details to the art fraud squad and we can help them."

"Noted."

From the woman's tone, Marina guessed the interview was over.

They signed themselves out, then stood in the police foyer. The weather had turned nasty. Heavy grey clouds hung in the sky.

The other bad news was the paparazzi waiting for them outside.

Damn, they'd found her.

Outside a police station and everything. What a horrible look.

Cooper found her hand and gave it a squeeze.

"Did you really mean it?" Marina looked up to him.

Cooper smiled.

"Don't tease me."

"I would never tease about something so important. Except, now I'm at a loose end because you haven't said it back."

Marina teased him. "I haven't?"

"Not yet."

"Wow! You're that confident I'm going to say it back?"

"Hmmmm. I wouldn't say confident. More like hopeful. My confidence is crashing by the second."

"I haven't said it yet, because you haven't groveled yet."

They were still standing in the foyer, as if waiting for the weather to improve before walking out - into a media storm.

"Hmmm" he pressed his lips together. "Only an idiot who didn't value what an amazing woman you were would stand here and say, 'what do I need to grovel for?', and I'm no idiot."

"I couldn't love an idiot," she teased back.

"Come on," he took her hand and they headed for

the front doors. "Let's get this out the way first and then we can have some privacy."

"What are you doing?"

"You'll see."

The wind blustered around them as they walked directly towards the media huddle.

As one the reporters started shouting questions to Marina.

Cooper interrupted them, "Ladies and gentlemen of the media, I have something to say."

They held their microphones out.

"Marina Shenko is completely innocent. She has already told the world she's innocent, but I also witnessed her honest reaction when she found out about her parents for the first time. She had absolutely no idea about any of it. Obviously, when your parents and loved ones are involved, you want to protect them. And then, because of who we are and the circles we move in, the perfect storm erupted where my mother, who is a prosecutor, and my father who is an art expert and assessor, became involved. It's a horrible coincidence, but the art world is a small one, and I should have seen it coming. Marina, I'm so sorry I didn't see it coming, and I'm incredibly sorry I didn't protect you more before you did the live interview. I should have told you, as soon as I knew, but I was a coward and I didn't want anyone to find out. I was hoping that if I shut my eyes it would all go away."

Maria's heart was nearly bursting out of her chest.

She stood still, frozen in the spotlight from the weather and the intensity of the situation.

Cooper added, "I could have prevented a lot of your pain if I'd been honest."

Tears came. Her nose sniffled as well, from the swirling wind and the emotions. A quiet little, "thank you" squeaked out. Then she said it again so that everyone could hear her, especially Cooper. "Thank you. And I'm sorry for being such an emotional basket case lately."

"Hey, we all get a few freebies."

Marina decided if Cooper could be brave - hey, it was in his surname after all - she could be as well. "I have a few things to say as well. I came to the police to let them know where I was, and that I'm available any time to answer their questions. I'm here to help. And you know what? I'll answer your questions as well. I'll stay as long as you need me to."

Voices crashed in on each other as they all asked at once.

"One at a time, please, I can't quite make them out. Oh, and by the way, this guy here?" She turned to Cooper. "He's amazing."

Exhausted, they made it back to Cooper's apartment. The media didn't follow them - they'd run out of things to ask and knew the storm was coming. Nobody wanted to be standing outside in this.

The wind howled down the streets, but they were safe and cozy in this apartment.

Marina pulled Cooper down onto the couch. "You were amazing today."

"Stop, you'll make me blush."

"The whole time I've been here, I've been on the back foot. Like I've been constantly hiding. I don't feel like I'm hiding any more, and that I don't even need to. I have you to thank for that. When you said all that stuff to the media . . ."

"I meant every word."

"I had to bite my tongue so hard not to blurt something out. I wanted to say it right there, in front of the world and everything. But then that would spoil it. The only person who needs to hear it is you. I really do love you Cooper."

Cooper looked speechless.

"I really do." Marina pushed on. "I think I have for ages, but I never had the courage to say it. That's probably why I reacted so badly after that live interview. I guess . . . if I didn't love you, it wouldn't have hurt so much."

"I never want to hurt you."

"Me neither."

Suddenly they were kissing, and it felt so right. When they eventually came up for air, Cooper said, "What took you so long to tell me?"

"You're going to laugh at me."

He pressed his lips together as if to hold a laugh back, then shook his head and said, "I promise I won't."

She snuggled into his chest. "I wanted it to be private."

His body shook as he held it together. Marina didn't, she let out the snortiest giggle and then wiped away a happy tear. "I know, right?"

"I'm laughing at myself, for not seeing what was right in front of me."

"Me too."

After some more wonderful kissing, Cooper asked, "This privacy thing, how long does it last?"

"As long as you want it to, I guess."

"I want it to last forever."

"You sure?" He didn't look sure.

"No, I'm not sure," and that was the truth. "But I really like it for now, so let's see how it goes?"

He gave her a heart-melting smile. "I really do love you, you know?"

Choked with emotion, Marina managed a crackly, "Back atcha, bae."

They kissed some more. Wonderful kisses that felt like the best drug ever. Marina felt so light she might fly away. When they eventually broke away, Marina wiped away another happy tear. "I feel like I've wasted so much time, being an idiot."

"Let's not waste any more time then," Cooper said.

A few days later, the effect of being with Cooper the whole time made Marina forget all about the outside world. It wasn't until Cooper's reminder went off about his next appointment that they realized the rest of the world had gone on spinning without them.

"A few week ago," Marina said, feeling a strange kind of understanding about her new situation, "I would have been going crazy not posting every day, feeling like my people needed me. I guess I was the one who needed them."

"You should be a psychologist."

"Lol."

"Did you actually say lol?"

"I really did."

While Cooper was seeing the counselor, Marina eyed the laptop on the table.

She wouldn't even turn it on.

She'd make a coffee and have a rest until Cooper came back.

OK, she'd turn it on, but only to check general news. Nothing personal.

OK so she logged in to her social network and saw a few posts.

How odd. It had only been a few days but she felt like she had so much catching up to do. And the bizarre thing was, she didn't really mind that she didn't have a clue what everyone else was talking about. A new movie was out. A new celebrity relationship (that did not involve her).

Which reminded her to check out the front door.

She could have fallen over at the sight. No media. Nobody waiting by the door.

Nobody cared about her.

Wow.

They really *had* left her alone.

Returning to her coffee, she clicked and watched a few trailers for upcoming movies.

OK, just a peek at the socials. She found a message from another influencer. A while back they would have been rivals. The girl was on her daddy's yacht. Surrounded by glossy timber and white leather, the update read, "Cannes is beautiful! Even in winter! I'm in a marina, Marina!"

It wasn't the furniture or the rounded portholes for windows which snagged Marina's attention. Or the joke about her name (which wore thin after the first three thousand times she'd heard it). It was the painting on the wall. A study of women dancing ballet, done in a cubist style.

Marina screen-grabbed the photo, cropped it to include only the painting and then tried a reverse image search.

Bingo. Marina had her answer.

Many more by the same artist were hanging in the National Gallery of Prague.

Marina replied, "Love the art!"

Would her friend take the bait?

She made another coffee and paced the room a few times. The clock said Cooper still had another twenty minutes before he'd be home.

The app pinged.

"It's gorgeous yes? & we didn't get it at your Dad's so it's legit!"

Marina had her doubts about that. Especially when she'd found others like it so easily. But she was starting to think the people who splashed their cash about, like her super-rich colleagues, didn't care much about real art, much less how to do a reverse image searches to see if others were already out there.

When Cooper came home, she showed him. "I wasn't on socials to post about myself, but I saw this and ... something's gone off in my brain. Maybe we could team up and be, like, I don't know, spotting art fraud in the wild or something?"

Cooper chuckled. "You mean trolling those Rich Kids of SocialPix?"

"Trolling is an ugly word. I call it social media due diligence."

It was time to say goodbye to Miss Beatrice, Pearl, Prithee and the chalet. While Marina didn't exactly think of her time here has 'fun', she had learned a few home truths about herself. Her bags were packed and everyone was standing around in an awkward way, not sure if she was going to give a round of hugs or merely walk out.

"Give me a moment," she said, heading back to the room.

The tiny room where the sun beamed in creating prison bar shapes with light.

She opened the window shutters and let the light in. Something glinted in the corner of her eye. Huh? It was a piece of jewelry on the top of the wardrobe. She reached for it and blew away the decades of dust gathered on it.

Another earring.

Well how about that?

Something rattled on the window. A chunk of dirt. She pulled the window open to see Cooper standing there waving up to her.

"Hello lovely distraction."

"Hello beautiful. Couldn't resist one last stone."

She smiled. "See you downstairs in ten seconds."

Closing the window pane, she took one last look around the poky little room with all its strange memories.

The she breathed in some fresh confidence, walked out and closed the door on that chapter of her life.

As another new beginning with Cooper loomed bright and sparkly ahead of her.

Ebony McKenna is an award-winning, bestselling author of young adult fiction.

EBONY MCKENNA, YA ROMANCE

The Summer of Shambles
    The Autumn Palace
    The Winter of Magic
    The Spring Revolution
    A Brugel Fairytale Treasury
    1916ish
    Robyn & the Hoodettes
    The Girl & The Ghost (winner, RWAustralia's
Romantic Book of the Year)
    Outback Yankee

NON-FICTION

Edit Your Own Romance Novel
    Get Your Book Into Australian Libraries
    The Ticking Clock
    Author Emails

Author Business College

She also writes regency romance as Ebony Oaten, and contemporary romance as Ebony Jean.

EBONY OATEN REGENCY NOVELLAS

Unsuitable Suitors series

1. Marquess and Tell
2. Me and Mr Jones
3. There's Something About Mary (Secrets of the Soho Club anthology)
4. Weekend at Baron E's (coming soon)
5. To All The Earls I've Loved Before (coming soon)

EBONY JEAN, CONTEMPORARY ROMANCE

Cupid Games
  Ripe for the Picking
  www.ebonymckenna.com

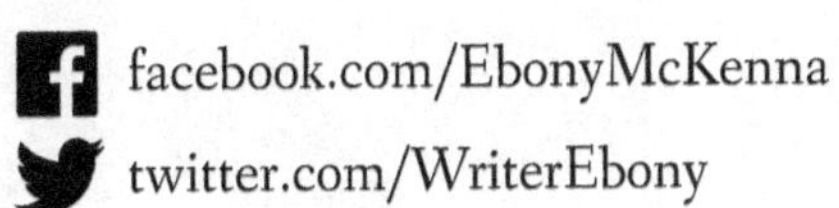
facebook.com/EbonyMcKenna
twitter.com/WriterEbony

BY THE PEALING OF THE BELLS

BONUS SHORT STORY

By The Pealing Of The Bells was originally published in *The Hauntings Of Livingstone Hall,* an anthology of ghostly short reads set on the cruise liner, Spirit of Bermuda, the most haunted ship on the high seas.

It was published in September 2019, long before Covid19 took over the entire planet, and with it the industry of ocean cruises.

Take it from me, don't ever go on a cruise with your mam. It's exactly the same thing as being stuck at home with your mam, but with added nausea.

All my friends are . . . well, they're in school. They're jealous of me because I'm 'cruising around the Caribbean having a great time'. Ha! I'd be in school right now, if they'd let me back.

Anyway, here I am, on a once-in-a-lifetime Caribbean cruise and all I can do is moan about missing out on regular life. Because I'm missing my friends, I'm missing the shops, I'm missing Instagram because Mam gave me a new phone for the trip that doesn't have data 'so we don't get billshock'.

I might even be missing my coursework.

OK, that's going too far.

Bermuda is really pretty. Palm trees everywhere.

Flowers galore. The buildings look as old as the Georgian towns back home, with their pastel painted walls. Quick selfie to show my friends where I am. That's right, can't send it until I can find Wi-Fi. Guess I can wait until I'm back on the boat. We sail tonight, and in the morning, I'll have another island to explore while Mam and her bellends, I mean, *bell ringers*, can bang on.

It's raining. Nothing like a good, Swansea drenching though. This is light rain; gentle and sweet, almost warm. Not-even-trying-to-rain rain.

Just as the thought, 'Something must be open where I can spend some time without spending too much money' crosses my mind, there it is up ahead.

A big, white colonial-looking building claiming to be an Aquarium, Museum and Zoo all in one. Adorable! There is an enormous pool out the front with seals! My day just got 300% better.

This museum slash aquarium slash zoo is deceptively huge inside. Oh yes! They have Wi-Fi. Nice one!

The aquarium-y sections are predictably crowded, but the old museum building looks like a good place to while away the rainstorm. There's a cosplayer in here, adding to the 'authenticity' of the experience. I'm not sure if he's supposed to be a pirate or just a shabby drunk. If he intro-duces himself as Jack Sparrow, I'm out of here.

He'll make a cute selfie though, so I sneak one in and . . . aww pig's poo! "You're not showing up in the photo!" He's right behind me and yet not on the phone screen. When I turn around to face him, there he is.

"At your service m'lady," he takes his shabby hat off and makes a clumsy bow. A broken feather falls off. With quick reflexes, he grabs it mid-air and slots it back in place. The broken quill rights itself.

"Just what I need. Another stupid ghost!"

P raise the angels, what wondrous fortune smiles upon me this day, that such a lady should enter my domain? She is wearing the sign of the bell on her ears and on a ribbon around her neck!

> *"By the pealing of the bells, 'till the sun in the east*
> *Gather all pieces, then ye shall feast!"*

Goodness, I am staring. Where are my manners?

"Allow me to introduce myself, Rufus Swain, at your service." Oh, blessed day to have finally arrived. My missing piece!

She fixes a determined expression as addresses me, "I don't need your service. You're a ghost. All your lot do is cause trouble!"

She turns to leave, but the maelstrom beyond the door halts her progress.

"My lady, do not depart. It is most inclement out of doors."

I must have that button on her scarf, before the pealing of the bells. I've come too far to fail.

"You're right, I'll need this," she says. Cool wind blows against my head as she grasps my sailing hat and places it upon her person. She takes two steps outside and the hat falls to pieces. "What the?" She cries out. "Is it made of tissues?"

I dash into the downpour and gather the scraps together, placing them upon on my own head.

"They . . ." her mouth opens and closes in a perfect imitation of a freshly caught bream, "Your hat's in one piece again!"

"Indeed. My lady, please step inside, this is no place to be conducting a conversation."

Meaning only to show good manners, I reach for her hand to lead her to safety. She swats me away, causing three fingers fly off into the interior of the museum. I so detest when that happens. At least they have not scattered to the four winds and sent me searching the gullets of seagulls this time.

"Gross!" the lady cries.

"Is everything OK in here?" A third party approaches, wearing the modern attire of the museum staff.

My angel lady dashes inside. I gather my distributed fingers and place them in position, where they knit into place.

Whole again.

Or very nearly so.

"You realise this museum is haunted, don't you?" My lady says to the curator.

"This is Bermuda honey, they didn't call it The Isle of Devils for nothing."

"Of course not."

She is thrilling to watch, gathering her composure in a far shorter time than I gather myself together most days.

"I came in here to get out of the rain," she begins.

The lights flicker. An alarm rings. My hands rise in surrender, "T'was not I!"

Are these the pealing bells? Am I too late to be whole once again?

The curator rolls her eyes and says, "The birds must be chewing the cables again."

CHAPTER THREE
LAUREN

This is so unfair. I can't be seeing ghosts and setting off fire alarms.

Not *again*.

What's this ghost going to make me do, burn the museum down? I'm getting out of here right now before they blame me for something I didn't do.

Again!

In the museum shop I buy a novelty umbrella (would a guilty person buy merch? Course not) and head out, following the road. There aren't that many roads here, so it's not like I'll get lost.

Good, there's the cruise ship's eight-seater golf cart. I flag it down and show them my passenger lanyard, then I climb in the back to the only spare seat. The view is foggy, thanks to the plastic blinds to keep the rain out.

The driver calls out, "Why are you sitting all the way down there?"

I'm about to reply, "Like I had a choice" when I look around and realise the golf cart is empty of the living, but massively crowded with the dead. And here's ramshackle Rufus sitting right beside me.

"I like it down here," I call back. I hate the way dead people make me do stupid things. Why can't anyone else see them, why is it only me?

Just as quickly as it bucketed down, the rain holds off and the sun shines. The golf cart stops at a sweet little old church on a hill. Fantastic spot for selfies.

The church bells ring out and Rufus gets this weird look about him, like he's having *an idea*.

"By the pealing of the bells," he says.

He said that back in the museum, too. Doesn't seem to be doing him any good.

Suddenly he's reaching for my chest. "Back off ya perv!"

The golf cart is nearby, so I race back and sit beside the driver for the rest of the drive back, not even bothering to check if Rufus Grabbyhands is with us.

When we reach the quay, The *Spirit of Bermuda* takes up all the view. It's a big boat. Or ship. I don't know their proper name, just that they're massive.

"Oh mighty vessel of the seas!" Rufus says behind me.

Has ignoring something until it goes away ever worked? Even with ghosts?

Then he says, "My lady, what incredible vessel is this?"

Will he and the rest of the ghosts on the golf cart be sailing with us? Surely it's too modern for – nope, my mistake. The rest of the ghosts stroll right up the gang plank, like they know exactly where they're going.

Am I going to gather a dead people fan club at every island we visit? In that case, I'll stay on board.

I am not raising the alarm. I am not pressing any buttons or activating door locks. My hands search my clothes for pockets, to keep them safely tucked away from touching anything. Getting kicked out of school was bad enough; getting kicked off the boat would be a complete disaster.

As we walk through one of the big mess halls, Rufus says in that old-fashioned sing-song voice of his, "Oh, that my eternal days of wandering shall soon be at an end!"

"Whatsat?"

"The final pieces are coming together. You my lady -"

"It's Lauren,"

"You, my dear Lady Lauren, the brooch on your person is one of the few pieces left to assemble. The bells on the hill. The light in the east which is the sunrise and people eating vast quantities of food. The feast!"

"You can't be serious?"

"The name of the vessel is sign enough, *Spirit of Bermuda*!"

I need to get away from everyone. "Please leave me alone." If returning to the cruise ship an hour or so ahead of sailing was supposed to offer peace and quiet, I have made a grave mistake. Pun absolutely intended. I can see dead people *everywhere*. They're walking arm in arm down the hallways – which are normally too narrow for regular people to walk that way, but ghosts don't have to worry about such peskyy things as solid walls.

They're not even pretending to keep out of my way, as if they can't see me. I want to pretend I can't see them, but as I march towards the dining hall, Rufus walking a few steps behind, ghostly ladies giggle and run away from each other, in a paranormal game of tag. A long-dead gentleman lifts his hat just now to acknowledge me and I. Cannot. Even!

I should go to my room and lock the doors and pour out a salt circle or something. Instead, my feet (and my hunger) take me to the nearest dining hall. The salty air has me craving chips. Instead of my favourite snack, I see the buffet filled with sugary cakes and slices for afternoon tea.

Come on Bermuda, chips aren't just a breakfast food!

Hmm, the tea though. Yes, a 'builders' is exactly what I need. I swipe my lanyard and grab a cup. Two bags for extra strength and the water is properly boiling. Good. Ooooh and they have ginger biscuits (Mam said something about ginger being good for upset tummies.)

Rufus can't drink the tea, which is probably just as well as a ghost drinking tea in here amongst us normal folk would really look weird.

Oh no, just when I thought this part of the ship would be safe, an armada of the undead wander in. I'm not going to get a moment's rest, am I?

There's a chance I could get some peace and quiet in one of the formal dining halls, so I head off in search of one. These formal areas are open for quiet gatherings and reading. Or convalescing, for those who overindulge the evening before.

It's lush in here. Velvet sashes and drapes on the walls, linen table cloths, crystal glassware. Plush, cushioned dining chairs. Silver cutlery that looks like real silver. This is the whole glamfest. Maybe I've walked into the first-class dining room by mistake? It wouldn't be the first time ghosts have made me do something embarrassingly stupid.

I don't remember it being this fancy last night. Then it hits me. Something shimmers just out of the corner of my eye, and the only way to see it is to look away slightly and catch it in my periphery.

There it is. This entire room has an extra layer of . . . *something* on it. This is the same place I had dinner last night, but the ghosts have taken over and covered everything with glamour.

Uh-oh, someone who looks a bit butlery from one of those costume shows on The Beeb comes my way. There's an Oliver-Twist looking kidlet walking along-side him.

"Good evening. I assume by your look of surprise . . ."

"Yes, I can see you," I confirm. "I can see all of you. You're everywhere. And I'm not happy about it."

"I am Hector, Head of Ghosts at Livingstone Hall. I wasn't aware there would be corporeal passengers on board with The Sight? I do hope we're not causing too much distress? We do try and keep to ourselves as much as we can."

"Rufus Swain, at your service," Rufus doffs his tattered hat.

"It's all his fault," I throw Rufus under the metaphorical bus. "He followed me from the museum. He tried to steal my scarf." When all else fails, appeal to authority. Maybe they'll kick Rufus off the boat and everyone else will vanish? The kidlet looks me up and down like he doesn't believe me.

"Allow me to explain," Rufus says, "The Lady Lauren and I have a misunderstanding. I require not the scarf, but the item nestled on it. It is a missing button from my jacket. It is the last missing piece and after that, at the pealing of the bells, I shall be whole again."

The kidlet says to Hector, "I used to think you were slow, but she takes the biscuit."

Hector frowns at the boy, then turns to me, "We cannot have fraternising causing distress amongst the passengers. The solution to this issue seems apparent. You could hand over the button and go your separate ways?"

"Well," my brain turns to custard. "I didn't realise it was . . . look, if some random came up to you and said 'give me that' would you give it over?"

"I did my utmost to explain my predicament," Rufus says.

"You grabbed!"

"You cast three of my fingers away!"

I stomp my foot. "It's a family heirloom!"

Rufus's shoulders slump. "It is merely a button from my seafaring jacket. It is worthless to you, yet beyond measure to me."

The kidlet speaks up again, "I bet he hasn't said the magic word."

Hector grins. "He's possibly lost his manners over the centuries."

Rufus looks ashamed for a moment. "Oh dear, it appears my manners have drifted into the trade winds!" Rufus's mouth then beams in a smile and he turns to me. "My dear Lady Lauren, I must apologise most sincerely for my ungentlemanly behaviour. If you would be so kind, would you *please* return the last piece of my ancient property so that I may be whole again?"

They're all looking at me like I'm the bad guy. I'm not the bad guy! "Oh all right!" I take it off and hand it over. "Now, you've all got to promise to leave me alone."

He affixes the button to his tattered jacket and something magical happens. His clothes repair completely, as if brand new. He straightens up and takes his hat off, making a sweeping bow. "Thank you my lady, I shall forever be in your debt."

Can you not?

Bells ring out through the deck. "The pealing of the bells!" The curse is indeed lifting, after all this time?

"Does that mean you're done, and you can leave me alone now?" Lauren asks.

I pat the button into place, but instead of corporeal, I feel only confusion. "I should be whole again, yet I am not. I do not comprehend . . ."

Lauren shrugs.

"Yet I heard bells!" I complain to nobody in particular.

The small lad beside Hector tilts his head, "That wasn't a bell, it was the ship's klaxon warning we'll be setting off again."

At which point, the Lady Lauren places her hand upon my form and protrudes her limb right through! If the ghostly persons around us could gasp, there would be some sharp intakes of breath happening. Alas, none of us has breath to spare. Except for Lauren.

"Sorry, mate. It's just that you have been dead for a while, so even if you died of natural causes you'd probably still be a ghost by now, right?"

CHAPTER FIVE

LAUREN

As fate would have it, Mam chose that exact moment to walk in with her bell ringers. "There you are! I was going to send the bursar after you to make sure you weren't trying to run away."

Haha, yes, because I'm the troubled teenager, of course. "No Mam, everything's fine."

She and the bell ringers set themselves up, covering a table with felt and testing their bells. It's a lovely practise scale, to warm their muscles and the brass, which can get out of tune in humid salty air.

Mam suddenly turns to me and asks, "Who's your friend? Will he be in the audience?"

"Wait, you can see him?" The words are out before I can haul them back in.

"I didn't have *that* much to drink at lunch," she shoots back.

Mam can see him. In fact, all the bell ringers can see him.

"S'cuse me," time to give Rufus another playful poke in the shoulder. This time my finger hits solid lad. A grin splits my face. "You're back!"

Rufus's face mirrors mine. "Huzzah!" He grabs me and spins me around. "The pealing -"

"- Of the bells!" we both say.

"Let's leave them to it, old man," the kidlet says. He and the butler get back to their ghostly decorating of the dining room.

Rufus eventually puts me down and we giggle and catch our breaths.

"How did the poem go again? Something about the sun in the east and a feast?"

> *"By the pealing of the bells*
> *'till the sun in the east"*

"Does that mean from now until sunrise?"
"I very much hope so. The next part is,

> *'Gather all pieces'"*

I join in the last line with him,

> *"And then ye shall feast!"*

We're both smiling at each other like we've solved a huge maths problem.

Rufus says, "It's been so long since I have eaten, I may even relish the taste of boiled mutton."

"You are in for a treat. Come with me and I'll introduce you to the best thing that's happened to British cuisine in the past two hundred years."

I take him to one of the casual buffets on the next floor. The air is thick with spicy aromas.

"Upon my word," Rufus says as he takes in the *bains maree*. "My eyes are watering almost as much as my mouth."

This will truly be a feast. "Rufus my friend, allow me to introduce you to the eighth wonder of the world. Chicken Tikka Masala."